Looking for Atlanta

Looking for
ATLANTA

A Novel by

Marilyn Dorn Staats

The University of Georgia Press

Athens and London

© 1992 by Marilyn Dorn Staats
All rights reserved
Published by the University of Georgia Press
Athens, Georgia 30602
Designed by Louise OFarrell
Set in 10/14 Linotype Walbaum
by Tseng Information Systems, Inc.
Printed and bound by Thomson-Shore, Inc.
The paper in this book meets the guidelines for
permanence and durability of the Committee on
Production Guidelines for Book Longevity of the
Council on Library Resources.

Printed in the United States of America
96 95 94 93 92   C   5 4 3

Library of Congress Cataloging in Publication Data
Staats, Marilyn Dorn.
Looking for Atlanta : a novel / by Marilyn Dorn Staats.
p. cm.
ISBN 0-8203-1470-6 (alk. paper)
I. Title.
PS3569.T1248L6   1992
813'.54—dc20   92-6016
                                        CIP

British Library Cataloging in Publication Data available

Excerpt from "The Old Man Who Said 'Why'?" from *Fairy Tales* by e. e.
cummings, copyright 1950 by Marion Morehouse Cummings and renewed 1978
by e. e. cummings Trust, reprinted by permission of Harcourt Brace Jovanovich,
Inc., and the Trust U/W Marion Cummings.

For Ethan, Natalee, and Ethan Lewis
In memory of Joe

Acknowledgments

To Karen Orchard, I express my deep appreciation. I am indebted to Renni Browne for her encouragement and help, to Charles East for his expert editing, and to Gail Galloway Adams and Molly Giles for their suggestions which led to revisions in the final draft.

For their support and insightful comments while I was writing *Looking for Atlanta*, I am grateful to the members of the Midtown Writers Group, especially Linda Clopton, Lila Howland, Bill Osher, Jim Taylor, Diane Thomas, Anne Webster, and Gene Wright.

And for showing me that I, too, could be a writer, thank you, Mother.

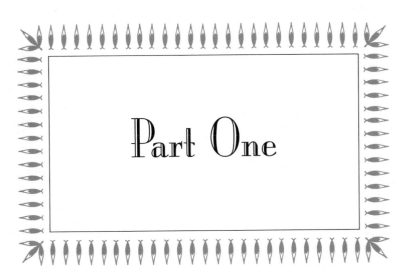

Part One

"Margaret Hunter Bridges! Have you gone and lost your *mind*?"

I ignore the peevish tone in Ida's voice and ease my way down to the side of the roof that overlooks the patio. Even from four stories above her head, I can tell she wants me to know she's mightily displeased. Her back is arched, her bosoms are heaving, and there is something about the way she is poking her chin out that reminds me of the time, more than thirty years ago now, when she played the role of Tinkerbell in the same sixth-grade musical at E. Rivers School in which I played the role of a dog.

"Well?" she calls up to me. "Are you going to explain what you think you're doing?"

No. What I am doing is writing down certain facts from the past in my new journal, I could tell her. But there's no talking to Ida Matthews when she is in one of her snits.

I begin crawling back to the top of the roof, to where Harold is lying half-sprawled beside the chimney. His knees still cradle the pitcher of drinks we borrowed from Ida's kitchen during the garden club meeting, but he's removed the white butler's jacket she made him wear, and he's spread it next to him for me to sit on.

"Don't get up," I tell him.

"No, ma'am," he says, slowly struggling to his feet. He points to my house across the street. "Jimmy be spying on us again."

"Yes."

A hand is raising the blinds in my bedroom window. The telescopic lens of my son's camera is seeing whatever it needs to see.

"Harold?" Ida shouts. "You get down from there this minute and bring that crazy woman with you, or I swear I'm going to fire you good!"

Harold grins and begins filling our plastic wine glasses with another round of Perrier and Chivas Regal. He's worked for Ida and Arnold Matthews almost as long as he's worked for me; he knows they're not about to get rid of family.

"Uh-huh," he says, lying down again. "Why does that boy keep watching us, Miz Margaret? What he be waiting for us to do?"

I don't answer. The roof is pleasantly warm in the afternoon sun, and our panoramic view of Arcadia Heights convinces me once again that the Matthews's yard is the finest in our subdivision. The pea gravel drive that winds its way up the rolling front lawn is lined with dogwoods and pink azaleas, and in the back, surrounding the patio and pool, Harold has planted hundreds of daffodils and tulips and those spiky blue flowers nobody knows what to call.

I raise my wine glass in a toast. "Here's to 'Spring the Sweet Spring,'" I say, naming the poem my daughter Meg recited so successfully last year on the stage of the Calvin Academy auditorium. "'Cold doth not sting, the pretty birds do sing . . .'"

"Yes, ma'am."

I prop my drink against the base of the chimney and open my leather-bound journal. The handwriting, I'm surprised to note, is odd. The usual loops of my *l*'s and *t*'s, the circle dots of my *i*'s and *j*'s, have somehow evolved over the past hour or so into meticulous block letters as unromantic as a divorce lawyer's.

OBSERVATIONS ON THE ROOF

April 17, 1981

3 P.M.

1. The mating call of the brown thrasher is a simple smack!

2. The veins of the flowering dogwood leaf curve upwards toward a smooth and wavy margin.

3. From twenty miles away, Atlanta's skyline looks . . .

"All right, you two!" Ida screams. "Those are antique cedar shingles you're sitting on! Remove your fannies this instant! Do you hear me?"

Yes, we hear her.

"Damn you!" she cries furiously. "I'm warning you for the last time, Margaret! If you're not down from there in the next ten seconds, I'm going to start counting!"

"Uh-oh," Harold says, chuckling.

"One!" Ida counts.

" 'Cuckoo, jug-jug, pu we . . .' " I call down to her.

"Two!"

" 'To witta woo!' "

I close my journal and look across the street to my bedroom window. The curtains are drawn. Jimmy is no longer there. *The fields breathe sweet, the daisies kiss our feet . . .*

"Three, damn it!"

I lean my head back against the chimney and stare up at a blank blue sky. I want to think of nothing at all. Not of my son, not of my husband . . .

" 'Young lovers meet,' " I continue doggedly, determined to quote to Harold every word of the stupid poem my daughter wasted so much of her precious time memorizing.

"Shit!" Ida screams.

And old wives a-sunning sit . . .

1

Certain facts from the past: In the beginning was Katherine. Katherine begat Margaret. Margaret begat Minevah. Minevah begat Leticia. Leticia begat Charlotte. Charlotte begat me: Margaret Hunter Bridges.

I was conceived in an upper berth of the old Southern Crescent. Or so I suspect. My parents' trip from Atlanta to New Orleans, which Daddy told my brother and me about one morning at the breakfast table when we were young, occurred nine months before I was born.

"Your mother," Daddy said, "used to find the sound of train wheels rolling over a track mighty, mighty stimulating." He gave Mother a little goose in her ribs. "Remember, Charlotte? G*alump*-a-*rump*. G*alump*-a-*rump*."

"Walter!" Mother cried out, so horrified at Daddy's lack of grace and dignity she almost knocked over her cup of coffee into my brother's lap.

Buford grinned. He was a couple of years older than I. He was old enough at eleven to have tried to convince me that our parents had gone all the way not only on the occasions of our conceptions but on several other occasions as well.

"G*alump*-a-*rump*," Daddy continued, looking up at our maid, Beatrice, who had come into the breakfast room to pour me another cup of Ovaltine. "You ever heard that sound?"

Beatrice tugged at the nylon stocking hiding her hair and went into her Aunt Jemima act, the one she often adopted to humor Daddy. "Yes, suh!" she said, hunching down and rolling her eyes. "Indeed I has, Mister Hunter."

"Oh, *Walter,*" Mother groaned as her orange juice went flying across the table. It spilled onto Daddy's open copy of *How to Win Friends and Influence People*, perhaps even splattering the very passage of Dale Carnegie's that had inspired Daddy's reflections on train rides.

" 'The famous Dr. Sigmund Freud of Vienna, one of the most distinguished psychologists of the twentieth century,' " Daddy had read aloud to Buford and me that morning, " 'says everything you and I do springs from two motives: the sex urge and the desire to be great.' "

"I don't know what gets into you sometimes, Walter!" Mother said angrily. She pushed back her chair so Beatrice could wipe up the juice. "Imagine saying such things in front of the *children.*"

But Daddy imagined many things. Some of them might even have been true:

Little girls who smile and speak softly, who go out of their way to be charming to every single solitary soul they meet, will grow up to marry little boys just as nice as their daddies. Little girls who whine and talk nasty and never think of anybody but themselves will end up like poor old Miss Riley next door, who has nobody to look after but her brother.

The Ten Commandments order us to never kill except in time of war or deer season or when electrocuting murderers and rapists.

It is wrong to say anything ugly about dead people unless they happen to be dead people like President Roosevelt, or Mr. Deakins down the street who died in the arms of a lady who wasn't Mrs. Deakins, or that two-faced Blake Washington fellow who tried to gyp your daddy out of profits on an entire month's worth of sales to the A&P Food Stores.

Never call a Jew a Jew to his face; it will hurt his feelings. The same for Catholics. (It is all right to call a nigra a nigra to her face because Beatrice is only a maid and she doesn't know the difference.)

If you swim in a pool other than at the Carriage Country Club, you get polio.

You should always honor your father and your mother and all the Atlanta relatives who came before you except your Grandmother Leticia, your mother's mother, who, if it were not for your daddy's generosity, would have died in the poorhouse.

"Oh, for heaven's sake, Margaret! You're old enough now not to listen to everything your father tells you," Mother said when I was twelve and joined the Buckhead Presbyterian Church and went into the kitchen after Sunday dinner to ask her if Daddy's interpretation of the Children's Catechism could possibly be true. ("Even though Jesus loves all the little children, Margaret, and suffers them to come unto Him, Jesus decided not to give some of the little children Grace before they were born, so they are predestined to burn eternally in Hell after they grow up and die.")

"Your father is a great man," Mother said, handing Beatrice a dry dish towel, "but *honestly*!"

"Honestly what?" I said.

Mother left the room without another word. She left without answering the question I've been asking myself in one way or another ever since.

———

Other facts from my past:

My father, Walter James Hunter, was the owner of the Hunter Baking Company, a business inherited from his grandfather and one which was going to be passed down to my brother if and when Buford ever decided to stop acting so lazy and good-for-nothing.

My mother, Charlotte Henderson Hunter, was the owner of *Mrs. Dull's Guide to Southern Etiquette*, a dog-eared book which contained Mother's favorite credo: "If something unpleasant is happening, pretend not to notice. To do otherwise would embarrass your guests and family."

We lived in a rambling two-story house in a northwest section of Atlanta called Buckhead. Because Mother went away to the tuberculosis hospital in Rome, Georgia, not long after I was born, during the first five years of my life I was raised mostly by Beatrice Jones, a brown-skinned maid who had a room in our basement. I don't remember what her favorite credo was, but she owned a rocking chair and a goldfish bowl and a recipe for peach fried pies that always brought forth the compliment from Daddy that her race was born to cook.

My brother and I attended E. Rivers School, which was within walking distance of our house, and then entered high school at Calvin Academy, a Christian preparatory school on the outskirts of Buckhead. After graduation, Buford ran away from home with dreams of making a million dollars as an itinerant fruit picker, and I entered Sweet Briar College to become a famous anthropologist or concert pianist or the president and founder of an Atlanta eleemosynary institution dedicated to saving the starving children of the world.

Something happened.

Buford became a millionaire, but I never became an anthropologist or a concert pianist. The only thing I've ever been the president and founder of is the Buckhead Garden Club. I don't even live in Atlanta anymore.

Listen. "Everything you and I do springs from two motives: the sex urge and the desire to be great."

Yes. These words are as true today as they were the morning I first heard them. These words are the reason why my husband Peter moved Jimmy and me out to the suburbs last year after our daughter Meg died. They are the reason why he left us there four months later and why, as soon as I walked into his downtown law offices two days ago to sign the separation agreement he insists he needs, I opened my mouth to say hello and realized I had become the one thing on earth I had never meant or wanted to become: a forty-three-year-old lapsed Southern Belle.

———

All the way into downtown Atlanta, I had tried to imagine what I was going to say to Peter. Once on a soap opera program my maid was watching in the kitchen while I fixed her lunch, there was a wife in much my same situation who thought she could convince her husband to return to her and the children by parking her Cadillac on a train track. Although she'd been in a coma since the preceding episode and her head was completely covered in bandages—only cracks for the eyes and nose and mouth—when her husband was brought to her bedside she roused herself long enough to tell him that if he didn't break off his affair with a certain female doctor, he would never see her alive again.

"*Whom* would he never see alive again?" I asked Annie D. "The wife or the female doctor?"

Annie D. was on her lunch break. She doesn't have to talk to me when she's on break, and by the time I remembered to watch another episode to find out if the wife succeeded in getting her husband back, an entirely different person was in the hospital bed.

"Leave Peter alone and he'll come home, dragging his tail behind him," said Ida. She was growing tired of all my complaints. She wanted me to start looking on the bright side. "Trust me. When he's had enough of this little Sydney Roberts bitch, he'll realize he's the last person on earth who could ever leave the bosom of his family."

The night Peter finally moved out for good, Ida sat me down on her living room sofa and handed me a book entitled *How to Make Your Dreams Come True!* "Visualize success," the book's author advised. "See it in your mind's eye."

What I was trying to picture as I drove downtown was Peter waiting for me on his hands and knees beside his desk. He would be hugging the family photograph Meg and Jimmy and I gave him two years ago for Father's Day, and the moment he saw me enter the room he'd beg my forgiveness. "Oh, my dear Margaret!" he'd cry, with tears in his eyes. He'd tug on my skirt. "I've been a total ass, darling. But, please! Give me one more chance."

Yes. With tears in his eyes. Or actually sobbing.

But as it turned out, it wasn't all that easy to imagine this scene in Peter's office because of the scenes I was seeing outside my station wagon window. Something had happened to Peachtree Street since the last time I'd been downtown. All my childhood landmarks had disappeared. The gray castle where I used to take piano lessons from a lady with a Pekinese was now a Chevron station. Maybe Gulf. And the office I used to dread to enter, where a man with rolled-up shirt-sleeves would adjust my back brace when I was slouching toward adolescence, had become the Kitty Kat Klub or the Beaver Bar or something. I didn't look. I stopped looking the minute I reached the corner where Mr. Baxter used to sell hot pistachio nuts in paper sacks and I realized somebody had not only removed Mr. Baxter but had changed the name of the street.

At the crest of Peachtree—where over thirty years ago my friends and I had watched Montgomery Clift sentenced to death for drowning a pregnant Shelley Winters, and where one hundred years before that the members of the Atlanta Ladies' Committee to Abolish Drinking Resorts, Gambling Dives, and Brothels had met in my great-great-great-grandmother Katherine's parlor and elected her president—I could find nothing left of my past except a huge hole in the ground. The hole was a half-block deep and a full-block wide. Around the hole was a cyclone fence with a sign that warned: HARDINGS WAS HERE!

Hardings was here? Who *was* this Hardings person? As far I could remember, there had never been a family by that name living in Atlanta since the day I was born!

I followed the muddy water flowing down the street from the hole in the ground until I reached the circles of ramps leading up to the roof of the Davison's department store parking lot. In the elevator going down, a possible rapist posing as a Cuban aluminum-can collector plopped his bag right down next to me. A black man with a nervous Adam's apple and a suspicious bulge in his coat pocket—perhaps he was the serial killer the police were looking for in the case of Atlanta's missing and murdered children!—began picking at his teeth with a switchblade knife.

I didn't look. Instead, I perused the message under the elevator's microphone and camera: "For your protection, your conversation and movements are being recorded."

The law offices of Willowford, Shags, Liebermann and Bridges are on the twenty-second floor of the Equitable Building. When I entered the reception area, I was dressed for the occasion. I was wearing new red boots and the pioneer skirt and blouse that the saleslady in Laura Ashley's had sworn I shouldn't have to live without. Ida had taken me to the beauty parlor the day before to get a man named Hal to cut my hair in a pageboy style—if there is still a style like that—and to dye the gray a strawberry blonde to go with my recent color analysis. ("You are *spring!*" trilled a delighted Ms. Lovehart, a cosmetologist who specializes in helping middle-aged ladies like Ida and me discover our true identities.)

As I approached the reception desk, I was very much aware of what my mother had told me over the telephone before I left the house. "Hold your shoulders up, Margaret," she'd said. "And remember, dear: It is impossible for anyone to feel sorry for a girl who smiles and has just had a professional manicure."

Peter's secretary is a Miss Grimsley. I'd never met her before—nobody from Atlanta goes downtown anymore—but when I was ushered into her office, I found her to be attractive in the exact same way a Doberman pinscher puppy is attractive: Young, sleek, alert. With perfect posture. She was studying her horoscope in the

Atlanta Constitution with the air of a woman who wants you to think this is just a chosen momentary idleness in a day otherwise crowded with last-minute appeals on behalf of an innocent client facing the electric chair.

In reality, Peter doesn't know anybody in jail. His clients wear pin-striped business suits or silk blouses with cameo brooches. The closest he ever comes to last-minute appeals are telephone calls late at night from clients who are having second thoughts about their divorce settlements.

"Yes," Miss Grimsley said, looking down at her appointment book and stabbing my name with the eraser end of her pencil. "Here we are. Margaret Bridges. Wednesday, April 15th. Eleven o'clock." She glanced at her watch before shifting the pencil to her right hand in order to give me a check mark for punctuality.

From the way she avoided looking me in the eye, I knew Peter had told her what I was there for. What I didn't know was whether or not he had told her any of the details.

"Have a seat, Mrs. Bridges," she said. "I'll just see if Mr. Bridges is free."

While she whispered over the intercom phone to Peter, I tried to decide how much I should tell her. Peter and I had been married a long time. Over twenty-three years. Only recently had I discovered that our marriage was doomed from the beginning.

"Or to be fair," I said to myself loud enough for Miss Grimsley to overhear, "perhaps the only thing doomed from the beginning was me."

And Meg, of course.

Also, my son Jimmy.

Also, my mother and father. My brother Buford.

Everything I had seen on my way down Peachtree Street. Everybody I had ever known or would come to know in my whole entire life.

Even Miss Grimsley's days were numbered. She deserved an explanation.

When she put down the telephone and informed me that Mr.

Bridges could see me now, I walked up to her desk. I wanted to tell her about Peter thinking he was in love with a young female medical doctor. I wanted to explain to her how Peter had these needs. The needs, he said, of any normal forty-six-year-old man.

"Yes, Mrs. Bridges?" Miss Grimsley asked, waiting for me to say something.

"And many more," I said. "Believe me, Miss Grimsley. Mr. Bridges has these needs, and many, many more."

Miss Grimsley pulled the newspaper closer to her and pretended to study her horoscope for loopholes.

"Protect your territory," I warned her, tapping Today's Starcast with my manicured index finger. "Forget about man, my dear. Be your *own* best friend."

———

Peter was standing behind his desk when I entered the room. He didn't exactly fall down on his hands and knees when he saw me. He didn't even look at me, exactly.

"So, Margaret," he said. He was ruffling through a pile of papers as though he were looking for something important. "How have you been?"

"Fine," I said. "I'm doing just fine, Peter."

I tried once again to think of something to say to the man I'd loved over half my life, but although my mouth was open, all I managed to do was flash him a silly, flirtatious smile. Besides, as I sank down in the chair by his desk, I realized that Peter no longer looked like the man I'd been married to. He was taller and thinner and younger. With broader shoulders. His eyes were now turquoise instead of brown, and on the top of his scalp he had these little red lines that reminded me of chicken scratchings.

I knew I needed to tell him something before it was too late, but what? What does a man with new contact lenses and shoulder pads and high-heeled boots and a face-lift and a hair transplant need to hear?

I decided to tell him about this article I'd read at the beauty parlor about brain cells dying off as we get older. "They're beginning to think there might be a slight outside chance that brain-cell deterioration does not happen in every single case," I said.

"Good."

The family photograph of Meg and Jimmy and me had been replaced by a picture of Peter and Sydney running hand-in-hand across a finish line with a banner above it that read: 10K HEART RACE! They were wearing matching valentine uniforms: red, white, and blue umbrella hats. Itsy-bitsy orange shorts with slits up the sides. Silver and purple jogging shoes. Undershirts that looked like they'd been crocheted in tea-dipped string. Through the crocheting I could see where they had covered up their nipples with Band-Aids.

While Peter was taking his seat, I studied Sydney out of the corner of my eye. Apparently adultery was more exhausting than I had imagined. It struck me immediately that here was a child who needed a mother. Someone to towel her off and fatten her up. Someone to remind her nicely that she ought to act a bit more vivacious when she was running around with a man, and for goodness sakes stop sucking on her hair.

"So," I continued, "if you stay active and optimistic and childish and all, Peter, you can keep on growing brain cells almost indefinitely."

"Yes," he said. "Here it is." He leaned across the desk and handed me the paper he needed me to sign. "I don't expect you to understand all of this—there's an awful lot of legal gobbledegook—but if you'd like me to explain anything, Margaret, I will. Essentially, it just means I want to be fair."

Ah. I looked down at my fingernails. Someone had chewed off some of the polish.

"Listen, Peter," I said. "You have half of your life ahead of you, and what with scientific progress and all, you could hope to have even more ahead of you than that. You know, Peter?"

He smiled the way a man does when a woman is telling him something he already knows, and then he said: "So, you don't have any questions?"

I didn't know where to begin.

Pleasepeterpleasepeterpleasepeterplease.

When I raised my head, I saw him looking past my shoulder.

"There you are, Miss Grimsley," he said. "Would you kindly bring in another secretary to witness this and then see Mrs. Bridges out for me, please?"

At her desk I remembered what else I'd wanted to tell Peter's secretary.

"Did you know, Miss Grimsley, that Sydney Roberts—the female medical doctor with whom Mr. Bridges engages in sexual intercourse—is only twenty-eight years old? Did you realize she is only nine years older than Mr. Bridges's own daughter would have been had she lived? When I allow that thought to elbow its way through my chest, Miss Grimsley, I want to howl. Or I am absolutely speechless."

Miss Grimsley looked down quickly at her appointment book and crossed off my name.

———

"For the record, Mrs. Bridges, what is your full name?"

"Mrs. Peter Scott Bridges, Jr."

"And you live at what address in Atlanta, Mrs. Bridges?"

"I live at 305 Tributary Way, Northeast."

"And your relation to the deceased, Mrs. Bridges?"

"Mother. I was the Mother."

"No crime," the policeman assured me the day after my daughter died. "No crime has been committed here."

2

As I pulled out of the Davison's parking lot, I wiped my eyes on the hem of my pioneer skirt and remembered there was no reason to hurry back to Arcadia Heights. Jimmy would still be at school taking his final exams before spring break, and Annie D. wouldn't need me to listen to her latest problems with Mister D. because she was leaving work early to talk to her parole officer.

I decided to drop by the Nearly New Shop in Buckhead, where I'd worked for many years as the volunteer manager until the Junior League found out I was over forty and made me become an inactive member—or what they optimistically call a sustainer. I knew all the girls still working there would be happy to see me again. I wanted to let them know I was always available to give them any advice they might need about pricing or window displays or repairing broken items donated by other Junior League members. I could remind them that some items ought to be priced the minute they come in. Others should be repaired by volunteers trained to repair broken items. "Items beyond repair," I'd been meaning to tell the girls, "can always be used to teach the new volunteers how to fix things."

But when I entered the shop the only volunteers I saw were too young to know who I was. They followed me around as though they thought I was a customer. I tried on a few old sweaters and tested an electric hair dryer, and then I introduced myself to a girl behind the counter and asked her if I could please borrow the telephone. "I've just remembered," I told her, "that I promised to call my good friend and fellow League member Mrs. Arnold Matthews as soon as I got out of a very important business meeting I had to attend downtown this morning."

"Yes, ma'am," she said in the kind of superior, pitying voice a girl uses when she thinks you're old enough to be her mother. "Yes, ma'am, Mrs. Bridges."

I dialed Ida's number, but nobody answered. I tried to call a couple of other friends, but the line was busy at Joyce Belinda's house, and Mary Earle's nurse refused to let me speak to her. ("Mrs. Kennedy is getting her beauty rest," Nurse Hatcher lied.)

Mother had already informed me she would be playing bridge all afternoon at the Carriage Country Club, and there was no point in calling Daddy. Since his stroke last spring, he's lost the ability to speak. Whenever he hears the phone ring, he picks up the receiver, waits for you to say something, and then slams it down angrily in your ear.

I thought about calling Peter, but I hadn't come up with anything meaningful to say to him yet. The next time I talked to him, I wanted to make sure I had something to say that would bring him to his knees.

The only other person I could think of to call was my brother. There was a good chance, I knew, that Buford didn't love me all that much anymore—almost the only time we ever saw each other was at my annual dinner every Thanksgiving for the past twenty years—but still, it was a sister's duty to inform her brother about her separation before he found out about it from somebody else. Also, Mother had mentioned that Buford was going to have a party on Thursday night and I wanted to let him know I was now free to do just about anything I needed to do.

Although my brother grew up too intellectual and rich to inherit the Hunter Baking Company from Daddy, he has managed to lead a fascinating life nonetheless. He is a professional psychic.

He is also, or so my mother has told me, a financial advisor. I have no idea whom he advises, unless it is his wife.

Babs is an authoress, which is why she's never had time to have any children. You'd recognize her pen name. She is the lady who writes all those novels about women from small towns emerging into full sexuality. Her bedroom scenes take place in used-car lots and under executive-room conference tables and, according to what Meg once told me with great hilarity, "on the back of a polo pony, Mom!"

I wouldn't know. To tell the truth, I've never had time to actually read Babs. I've only had time to pretend to read her.

Anyway, I called Buford and I knew immediately that I'd gotten him at an inconvenient moment. He said hello in the tone of voice a man always uses when you've gotten him at an inconvenient moment.

"Buford?" I said. "This is Margaret."

"Margaret?"

"Yes."

"Uh-huh. What can I do for you, kid?"

There was nothing he could do for me, I answered. "I just thought I'd call and see how you and Babs are getting along, Buford. If you have a minute, though . . ."

"We're doing great."

I could hear somebody laughing in the background, somebody playing music from one of those countries where the natives don't eat cows.

"Also, Buford," I said, "I thought I'd let you know that I've been downtown today and—"

"That's swell. I wish I could hear about it sometime."

"—and you'll never guess what they've done to the old Coca-Cola sign that used to tell the time of day!"

"Yeah?"

"They've torn it down! And where the Loew's Grand Theater used to be, there's nothing left but a huge hole in the ground with a cyclone fence around it that says HARDINGS WAS HERE!"

"Huh."

"And Mr. Baxter is gone. Remember how we used to take the bus downtown every Saturday and buy hot pistachio nuts from Mr. Baxter on the corner? And then we used to walk down the sidewalk, hiding the sacks inside our pocketbooks so the people at the Loew's Grand Theater wouldn't know we didn't like their popcorn? And we used to sit on the front row that time in *Rear Window* and scrunch way down in our seats and try to look up Jimmy Stewart's leg cast?"

"No."

"Yes, Buford. You'd remember if you saw that hole in the ground. It was on the exact same spot where our great-great-grandmother Margaret opened Atlanta's first dancing school."

"Who?"

"The first Margaret. You remember."

"No. I have no memory of her whatsoever."

The music in the background was growing louder. "So, listen. Buford? How is everything with you and Babs these days?"

"Fine, kid. I'll tell Babs you called. It was good talking to you."

"Also, Buford, I wanted to let you know that I visited Peter at his office this morning."

"Uh-huh."

"And we've decided to become estranged. Peter and I were thinking that twenty-three years is a long time to stay married without becoming estranged for a while. You know?"

"Yeah?"

"There's every reason in the world to believe this is just a temporary arrangement. Peter needs to have these needs right now, and I don't seem to have any needs. That's the trouble with me, Peter says."

"Well, that's terrific, kid. Just temporary, huh?"

Buford said something else then, but I couldn't catch the words. The music in the background drowned out his voice. I wondered who might be talking and laughing and playing intellectual music in Buford's house at two-thirty in the afternoon in the middle of the week.

"So. That's about all I called to tell you," I said. "And also, I thought you might be interested to know I'm free now to do just about anything I might like to do. If you and Babs ever want to get together sometime—have the neighbors over one night for a party or something—I'd be happy to join you."

"We'll do that, Margaret. And keep in touch, kid. I really mean it. Keep in touch."

I stood behind the counter in the Nearly New Shop for a long time. After a long, long time I decided to wander around the store again and look for something to need.

———

"What I thought that might be," I told my yardman when I got back to Arcadia Heights, "was a talking doll like the one I bought at the Nearly New Shop when Meg and Jimmy were children. Not long after you came to work for us. Remember?"

Harold was in the backyard spreading cow manure around the new azalea bushes. He is a tall, lanky man with stooped shoulders and a pink jagged scar that runs down his face from his ear to his chin. I don't know how old he is—it's almost impossible to tell with black people—but I've known him all my life.

He used to drive a horse and wagon for my father's baking company. On summer mornings when he was in our neighborhood selling cinnamon buns and yeast rolls still warm from the oven, he would sometimes let Beatrice boost me up on the seat beside him, and after she'd climbed in the back he would hand me the reins and let me drive us all the way to the end of the street. When the company stopped home deliveries, Harold began working inside the plant as a packing boy. Fifteen years ago, when Daddy finally sold the family business to a conglomerate based in New Jersey, Harold came to work in my yard.

"The nurse doll," Harold said, picking up his shovel. "Yes,

ma'am. Had a tape recorder inside her. I recalls her, I sure enough do. Lord, she could talk all right. What you used to call that voice in that doll, Miz Margaret?"

"Grandmother Leticia."

"Uh-huh. Old Grandmother Leticia! Jimmy and Meg be asking me all the time to come listen to what she be saying next. Used to keep it in their Secret Room under the staircase. That's right. She be a *tall* doll."

"Three-foot-two." I reached into the wheelbarrow and grabbed a handful of manure. "She had a missing index finger."

"I remember."

"And one eye that never closed. I used to love that doll, Harold. I could tell Meg and Jimmy everything they needed to know without them ever finding out it was just their mother talking. Because of that doll, Harold, I always secretly believed my children were going to grow up to be just a little bit smarter than other mothers' children. You know?"

He nodded, but he didn't answer.

As I watched him shovel another load of fertilizer from the wheelbarrow and aim it toward a raw area around the bushes, I realized he was upset about something. I wondered if he was thinking about how much nicer our yard had been when we were still living in Buckhead. Now, instead of oak trees and shaded rock gardens, we had a flat square lawn baking in the sun with nothing on it except a few small trees propped up with stakes and string. Instead of crumbling brick walkways winding through clumps of perennials and wild flowers, we had this poor beginning of an azalea bed, a few jonquils and tulips planted inside a neatly edged semicircle. Hard red clay. Straw brought in by a truck instead of raked from under sixty-foot pines.

And Mr. Bridges hadn't built us as fine a house as Mr. Matthews had built for Mrs. Matthews across the street. I had long ago quit trying to explain there was nothing personal in this. Arnold Matthew's conception of "Idavillea" as a modern Tara had emerged concurrently with his conception of developing the old Middlebrooks estates into Arcadia Heights. "He'd been just driving along U.S. 41," Ida told me, "when he saw the For Sale sign hugging the highway. Honestly! After he drove onto the access road and came upon that beautiful Greek Revival manor home Rebecca Middlebrooks moved into as a bride in 1877, he couldn't hardly wait," she said, "to turn everything into an authentic southern subdivision."

"Razed, but not forgotten," Arnold likes to joke about the reproduction of the Middlebrooks mansion he built for Ida on the foundations of the original. He points with the pride of the preservationist to the beveled glass windows and the Corinthian columns he managed to salvage.

"And some of them cedar shingles," Harold often reminds me, sneering at the idea of a man so arrogant he will tear down a house, yet keep the roof above it.

"Uh-huh-*huh!*" Harold was muttering now. He stamped the last shovelful of cow manure into the hard red clay. "You oughtn't to be working out here without your gloves, Miz Margaret. And look at you! Wearing your good dress-up clothes."

"I had to go downtown."

"Yes, ma'am. Annie D. done told me." He looked past my shoulder, then shifted his eyes to the ground. "I sure be sorry. Mister Bridges is a good man. *Smart* man! Don't you worry none, Miz Margaret, he'll be coming back. Uh-huh. He loves that boy of his too much."

The sound of Jimmy's stereo suddenly blasted from the window of his upstairs bedroom. *They won't take me! They won't break me!*

I turned and headed toward the house.

"That's right!" Harold called after me. "I remember. That doll could talk, sure enough!"

I tossed the separation papers on the kitchen counter and glanced at the clock above the microwave oven. 3:58 P.M. In another hour and two minutes, it would be the official cocktail hour. Nobody would say a word against me if I fixed myself a drink.

My favorite drink is a Muddy Waters: milk, a sprinkle of nutmeg, and two ounces of rum. While I got out the ice, I read the message Annie D. had left for me under her Smiley Face magnet on the refrigerator.

"MURDER."

I shook my head and sighed. One of her soap opera programs must have been interrupted by an announcement of yet another body found in the case of Atlanta's missing black children.

I took my drink into Peter's study and turned on the television set, but there was nothing on any of the stations except reruns and cartoons and a couple of women being interviewed about orgasms. Through the window, I saw Harold plodding down the driveway to catch the MARTA bus back into town. He was stooped over, arms dangling at his thighs, and his head led the rest of his body, as though he were using his bald scalp to bayonet his way through enemy air.

I got up from Peter's chair and went and stood by the window so I could watch Harold cross the street. As he joined the other maids and yardmen waiting at the bus stop at the bottom of Ida's driveway, I wondered why he had allowed Ida and me to uproot him to the suburbs. He was too old to be taking a twenty-mile trip twice a week. He belonged back in Buckhead, working in the yard of an old clapboard house that had been added on to so many times it had no particular style except its own.

The radiators whistled in that house. The pine floors sang. It was a block from my childhood home. Our neighbors, for the most part, were people I'd known all my life. Or they were people, like Peter and me, who had moved into Tributary Hills when their children were little and had remained because they were as charmed as we were by the giant oak trees that formed canopies over the winding streets, and the sidewalks that were wide enough for two bikes to pass, and the small park at the south end that had a tributary of Peachtree Creek running through it past sliding boards and swings and weathered picnic tables.

Favorite neighborhoods all alike; only the names on the mail-boxes different.

Awakening to the thump of the morning newspaper landing on the third step of the front veranda, where a series of Thompson boys had aimed it for more than ten years. Cooking supper to the sounds of old Mr. Frawley parking his rattle-chug Oldsmobile in the garage, slamming the car door and hollering, "Maud! I'm home!" Falling asleep at night to the tinny plunks of Mrs. Dahlbender's out-of-tune piano.

Children were everywhere. Riding their skateboards down our driveway. Climbing the mimosa trees in our backyard. Playing Batman and Robin in the woods across the street. I'd stand at my kitchen window and watch them running single-file down the embankment into the same fine and private place where years earlier Buford and I had played Tarzan and Jane, the Battle of Peachtree Creek, Cowboys and Indians.

"Remember, Buford?" I'd asked at the last Thanksgiving dinner, the one I gave in my new suburban house that smelled of fresh paint and wet plaster. "Remember how all of us were Creek Indians at heart, even though the tribe you and I loved in the home movie Grandmother Leticia gave us for Christmas that time was not a Georgia tribe but some kind of weird western breed?"

It was a silent movie called *The Besieging*. Indians with black and white paint on their faces were riding the warpath against a pioneer family traveling in a covered wagon. Their roly-poly chief wore a feathered hat so heavy it kept jerking him sideways and backwards in a neck-cricking, mouth-gaping *Aieeeyee!*

"Remember the way we always thought the chief's pinto pony was suspiciously small to carry the weight of such a man and such a hat, Buford?"

"No," my brother said. "I have no memory whatever of that, kid."

"Yes. And when the Indians started whooping it up around the

wagon, the heroine—the daughter of the family—would most as-
suredly have been scalped had not a poor imitation of Tom Mix
come galloping to the rescue?"

Buford and I were always on the side of the Indians. We figured the heroine deserved to be scalped. Certainly her cries of
"Help! Help!" could not be taken seriously; they flashed across
the screen in an overly dramatic, florid script that made her plight
seem ridiculous.

"Help!" she would silently scream, her head peering anxiously
out of the opening of the covered wagon. "Help! Help!" she would
cry, her hands cupping her mouth before dropping to grip the ribbons of her bonnet. She never bothered to glance at her poor dog
crouching outside on the front seat of the wagon, shivering with
fright.

"Forget the girl!" we'd yell at the screen when the imitation
Tom Mix finally galloped through the circling Indians. "Save
the puppy!"

And we'd beg Daddy to run the movie backwards through the
home projector so we could see the heroine in peril once again
before we ran out of the house to play mumbley-peg in the backyard near the abandoned Victory Garden, or to play statues under
Mr. Dahlbender's hose, or to join the neighborhood children in
the park where every fall our parents raked oak leaves into huge
piles. While our fathers drank beer out of brown bottles and
talked about Nuremberg and Jackie Robinson, while our mothers
spread out the picnic suppers, we'd leap into the leaves and bury
ourselves. We'd burrow tunnels through the piles and plot our
someday-getaways to magical places far beyond our little Buckhead world.

Years later, when Meg and Jimmy were growing up, I'd join
the neighbors in the park in early spring for three-legged races
and sack races and egg-in-a-spoon races. For hamburgers and
roasted marshmallows. For the hot mulled cider Mrs. Simpson
had been making for me since I was a little girl.

"I don't understand," I told Peter the morning he showed me

the brochures of Arcadia Heights: Atlanta's Most Exclusive New Suburban Subdivision. It was an early Saturday in September. Jimmy was still asleep upstairs, and Peter and I were in the kitchen pretending nothing had happened to turn us into two people drinking coffee and talking to each other with the courtesy and caution of new acquaintances. I looked away from this man with gold-rimmed glasses and dark hair thinning across the front of his scalp, and I looked down at the brochures spread across the counter. "I don't see the point," I said. "Why do we want to move away from here?"

"Arcadia Heights will have its own tennis club and swimming pool," Peter said. "You'd love it, Margaret."

All the houses were being built by Arnold Matthews, in styles that recalled an earlier, more genteel and aristocratic South. We'd have our choice of eleven different floor plans. "Everything top-drawer," Peter said.

I hunched into myself and tried to figure out what he was trying to tell me.

"Look at this!" he said, handing me a color Polaroid of a large unfinished Williamsburgy house stuck in the middle of a red clay lawn that was as raw as a popped blister.

"I don't know," I said. "I don't think we want to move away from here. Do we?"

"For God's sake, Margaret. We're still living in the same decaying neighborhood you've lived in all your life. This house is falling apart. The radiators hiss. The floors creak. The plumbing groans. Everything is moldy and damp because of the goddamned trees that block out the sun. All we'll be doing for the next three months is raking up leaves."

We carried our mugs of coffee into the breakfast nook. Peter sat across from me and rubbed his eyes with the heels of his palms. His elbows dug into the worn formica table top.

"Margaret," he said hopefully, "wouldn't you like something new? This house must be sixty-five years old by now."

"But we *like* old houses, Peter."

"The only people who like old houses are all the damned plumbers and electricians and roofers who make their livings off them."

"And we *hate* all these show-and-tell subdivisions Arnold Matthews is developing. Places like Arcadia Heights are offensive, don't you think? I mean, they have absolutely no character, no sense of history to them." I picked up the Polaroid, handed it back to him. "I don't see how anybody in his right mind could compare this architectural fake to the house we live in now."

"We live in a crypt."

"But *Peter* . . ."

"We live in a crypt surrounded by other old and depressing crypts. And old and depressing people. Jesus! Don't you think it's about time we stopped wallowing in the past?"

Ah, well. I looked away from the pain in Peter's face. Yes. Meg had been dead since April. Five months and eleven days. We'd had our grief, but now it was time to pack up our memories and become happy pioneers. Modern homesteaders. Settlers in a wilderness called Atlanta's Most Exclusive New Suburban Subdivision. A place where the neighbors wouldn't know us, where they would not bring over ham and turkeys, casserole dishes, buckets of tears. Where they would not sit for weeks in our living room consoling themselves with platitudes that might or might not be true: "Time heals all wounds" . . . "There is a reason here we cannot see" . . .

Peter interrupted my thoughts. "Try and understand, Margaret."

His voice was plaintive, and I quickly raised my eyes from my lap. I expected him to be looking at me, but instead he was staring at the lopsided face that Meg or Jimmy had once carved into the table top when they were young.

"I do understand," I said quietly. "I understand we'd be strangers. Is that what we really want, Peter?"

He said nothing. He began tracing with his fingers the outline of the lopsided face.

I watched myself sitting politely across the table from him, waiting for him to continue. *Oh, Peter.* My mind flooded with emotions I'd been unable to feel for him for months: Love. Pity. Despair. *Dearest Peter.* Because it wasn't the old radiators and the creaking floors in our house he minded. It was the upstairs bedroom with the flowered wallpaper and the four-poster bed and my grandmother's vitrine filled with Meg's collection of music boxes. It was the Secret Room under the staircase where Meg had played with her favorite dolls when she was young and read her favorite novels when she was older. It was all the reminders of missed opportunities, misguided intentions, misfocused ambitions.

Yes. We needed to get the hell away from Mr. Frawley next door who could remember the red-headed toddler who used to push her baby brother down the sidewalk in an antique carriage so high she had to push it on tiptoe. We needed to live some place where Mary Earle and Wally Kennedy were not around the corner to recall an eight-year-old girl with stringy legs and untied shoelaces ringing their doorbell to give them kittens abandoned in the woods, to sell them Girl Scout cookies and magazine subscriptions and tickets to the annual Calvin Academy May Day Festival.

It wasn't the patches in our dining room ceiling or the drafts coming through the warped windowsills in our bedroom that made Peter want to run away from Buckhead. It was the front porches of our neighbors that summer Meg grew taller than her father, matching him stride for stride as they jogged down Tributary Way before breakfast. It was the men on those porches and the way they would look up from the newspapers they were retrieving and wave at this teenaged girl with the long legs and the slim body, the way they would suddenly remember the feeling of being young, of being cocky with the strength of it.

And it was our own back porch stoop, where Meg often did her homework in the early evenings of that last bittersweet spring, where she would pile her schoolbooks at the feet of her latest boyfriend, *BobbythisBobbythatBobbyBobbyBobby*, and look away from his face only long enough to welcome her daddy home from the office.

Yes. That morning he showed me the brochures of Arcadia Heights, Peter needed to get the hell away fast. He needed to get the hell away from knowing eyes, from veiled expressions, from everyone who had stood in circles of fear and sadness that afternoon when a girl's body was brought out of the woods across the street. ("I don't understand," Mary Earle kept crying. "We used to swing on those vines all the time when we were her age. Why did God *do* this to Meg?")

He needed to get the hell away from the sight of a green plastic body bag being loaded onto a stretcher and lifted into the back of a police ambulance. ("They say she'd been dead for hours," we heard someone whispering behind our backs. "What I'd like to know is where was her mother? Why did it take her so long to know her child was missing?")

Oh, my God.

And we'd turned away from the ambulance and the police car driving slowly up a winding street canopied by oak trees. *Oh, please dear God.* And our neighbors had turned away from the boy racing into the house and the father racing after him and the mother standing alone in the middle of the street. *Runorstayrunorstayrunorstay.*

Peter would come home from work at night and find these neighbors sitting in our living room. Ida or Mary Earle or Joyce Belinda. He would nod, smile, and then without a word walk back to the kitchen to fix himself a drink. And they would leave immediately, making their awkward exits with hurried kisses, embarrassed embraces, saying nothing about the sound of Peter's television set in the den turned up loud enough to drown out our *whys*, our *if onlys*.

I would find him sitting in his leather armchair staring at the evening news. Or I would find him upstairs in Jimmy's room, the two of them turning as one to see me standing in the doorway, feeling like an intruder. And I would wait for Peter to accuse me, for my son to accuse me. To ask me why I would sit around all afternoon crying with women in the living room, nursing my grief and telling them things that were none of their business.

Because a man doesn't tell. A man holds his grief inside himself until a morning in September when he can sit in a breakfast nook and pour out his enthusiasm for a sauna there is still time to add to an upstairs bathroom, a sundeck there is still time to extend across the back of a porch.

"We'll install a Jacuzzi," Peter was saying. "You'll love it, Margaret. You'll have Ida for a neighbor again. And the Marchesons—he's the new president at First National—just bought the Queen Anne on the corner, and this guy Jim Rogers I met the other day at Downtown Rotary is looking into the Colonial . . ."

"But I don't know the Marchesons or Jim Rogers."

"Well, you can meet them, honey. They sound like the kind of people you'd like."

"I'm too old to make new friends. I have trouble finding enough time to be good to the friends I've already got."

Peter wasn't listening. "Look around you," he said in the voice of the divorce lawyer who has finally gotten his client's attention and can now explain what is best for everyone concerned. "Poor old Mr. Dahlbender spends every afternoon of his life standing in his backyard watering the grass with a hose gripped at his crotch. Jesus Christ! We won't have to be polite to that senile Mrs. Simpson any longer. Think of it! No more having to thank her for bringing us yet another milk bottle filled with that god-awful syrup she calls 'hot mulled cider.' "

I listened to his chair scraping against the floor and looked up in time to see him walking back into the kitchen. I followed him to the doorway and watched him lift the coffee pot from the stove. He lifted it slowly, like an old man testing to make sure it wasn't too heavy for him to handle, set it down again, and walked over to the window.

"Peter . . ." I started toward him, ready to tell him everything was going to be all right. I tried to put my arms around him.

"And Mr. Frawley next door," he said jerking away. "We can have dinner at night without having to listen to him hollering out, 'Maud! I'm home' to a wife who's been dead three years." Peter gave a short laugh that came out like a sob.

"Oh, Peter," I said, but he had already turned from the window and was on his way out of the kitchen. I followed him as far as the dining room. I heard the front door's soft click, the swollen *thump* as it closed behind him.

"Please, Peter," I whispered to him that night in bed. "I'm not sure moving away is the answer. Don't do this to us, Peter. I need this house right now. Jimmy needs to be around the people he's known all his life. Okay?"

Peter is a sound sleeper; he is somewhat hard of hearing. Noises like a faucet dripping or pine cones falling outside the window in the dark, or someone perhaps hiding in the room—I thought I heard a faint *whoosh!* under the bed—never bother him at all. He always wears a nightshade over his eyes so the light from his alarm clock won't disturb him, and all night long the humidifier hums through his dreams.

In my own dreams that night I was swinging on this vine as big as a man's arm in the woods across the street. They were the woods where Ida and Mary Earle and her twin sister and I used to spend the daylight hours of our summers. Where Buford and his friends used to build tepees by cutting down pine saplings, four to a tepee, tying them with vines and then covering them over with pine needles.

When we were children, we had known the spirits of the Creek Indians who had been driven away from those woods by the evil White Man: there was a deep cave dug by squaws in the creek bank near the train trestle. We knew the ghosts of the seven thousand soldiers killed in those woods on a single afternoon: a Civil War cannon barrel lay half-buried in the creek bed near the pine grove where the hoboes built their fires. Whenever we wanted to, we could find minié balls, arrowheads, belt buckles, and shards of what we took to be Indian pottery. And when we weren't playing

Cowboys and Indians (the losers having to play the swaggering cowboys) or War Between the States (the losers having to play the swaggering Yankees), we played Tarzan and Jane.

Except in this dream I wasn't a child, I was a middle-aged woman. And I was swinging on a vine as big as a man's arm when suddenly I looked up and saw a girl falling out of the sky. I quickly swung down to save her, to catch her and cradle her in my arms. But I could never push the dream that far. For hours I was never able to save the girl, or not save the girl.

In the middle of the night I bolted straight up in bed and reached out my hand to find Peter. "Tell me!" I cried. "If I'd warned them about those vines a long time ago, do you think she'd still be alive?"

"No crime," Peter mumbled in his sleep. He put his fists over his eyes and turned his back on me. "No crime has been committed here."

I lay beside him in the dark and tried to lull myself into the dream again by matching my breathing with his. *There, Margaret.* When I realized I was trying to match the rhythms of a man sobbing, *There now, Margaret,* I got out of bed, pulled on my old flannel robe, and went into Jimmy's room.

Jimmy had fallen asleep in his clothes. He was lying on top of the quilt, his right arm dangling off the side of the bed. I brushed his dark hair from his forehead and arranged his arm across his chest. Then I wandered downstairs to the kitchen, fixed myself something warm to drink, and went outside to sit on the back porch stoop.

There was no moon. There were no stars. Only the lights of an airplane that was moving slowly across the sky.

Help.

Mrs. Dahlbender next door was playing her piano. The windows of Mr. Frawley's house were dark.

Oh, please, dear God. Help.

I huddled in my robe and waited until the plane had passed over the roof of my parents' house a block away and droned out of sight. I waited until Mrs. Dahlbender's stiff, determined fingers reached the end of "Whispering Hope." Until the light came on in Mr. Frawley's bedroom and a shadow behind the curtains began pacing back and forth, back and forth.

Damn it, God. Come help us.

I waited on the back stoop until I grew tired of watching the florid script of my silent prayers fall out of my mouth and melt into the steam rising from Mrs. Simpson's hot mulled cider.

―――――

"Poor old Mr. Frawley," Harold said one morning while we were planting tulip bulbs in six inches of potting soil he'd spread on top of hard red clay. "Ain't seen him since we moved out here to the suburbs. Nor Mrs. Dahlbender, nor Mrs. Simpson, neither. Huh. Made that syrup stuff she call cider. Uh-huh. I sure be agreeable with Mr. Bridges about that syrup, Miz Margaret. Meg give me some to pour down a yellow jacket hole one time and it about killed a foot of grass."

Harold eyed the spacing in the tulip bed and rearranged a bulb. "Yes, ma'am," he continued, sitting back on his heels. "Killed the yellow jackets, too."

I closed my eyes and tried to visualize Meg handing Harold the jar of cider. I could imagine Harold kneeling on one knee to aim the syrup down the hole, but the girl standing behind him had no features, no shape.

" 'No crime,' " I murmured, giving Harold another bulb to plant. "They told us no crime had been committed."

"Why, Miz Margaret!" he answered, his voice filled with sorrow and consternation. "That's the truth exactly. Don't you ever go believing nothing different."

3

"It is now five o'clock. Do you know where your children are?"

I turned away from the window in Peter's study and walked across the room to switch off the television set. *Newswatch* had ended with its usual public service announcement, but there had been nothing about another child's body having been found. Only a parade of prominent blacks passing through Atlanta to give interviews on the reasons behind the current serial killings: poverty, racial discrimination, inadequate housing, overcrowded schools, the South's long history of ignoring the needs of minorities.

I was back in the kitchen about to fix myself another Muddy Waters when the phone rang.

"How did it go?" Ida asked before I had a chance to open my mouth and say hello. "What happened between you and Peter?"

Ah, well. I had no idea how to answer such questions. They were, in fact, the questions I'd been asking myself for over twenty-three years.

"So? Did you see him?" Ida said.

"Yes."

"And? What did he say?"

"He said he's picking Jimmy up tomorrow after work to take him to Lake Burton for the weekend. He'll bring him back on Monday."

"That's it? That's what you're telling me happened? You went downtown to discuss a separation agreement, and what you did instead was make arrangements for Jimmy's weekend trip?"

"And guess what, Ida. Peter keeps a picture of himself and Sydney on his desk. She has long blonde hair. No hips. Small boobs. They were running together across the finish line of the Heart Race. Holding hands. Can you believe it?"

"Yes. Now listen to me. What did—?"

"And Peter's gotten a hair transplant. He has these little stitches running across his scalp, and the top of his head looks kind of like he's wearing one of those rubber caps they use in the beauty parlor when they're frosting you. You know? The cap with the holes all over it and the little pieces of hair sticking out? His head kind of reminded me of that. And he's wearing contact lenses. Turquoise. I think he's trying to pretend he's—"

"Be quiet, Margaret. I can't understand what you're saying for all the talking. Did you—?"

"—Paul Newman."

Ida sighed. "You chickened out, didn't you? I swear. You promised me you were going to tell him if he didn't stop screwing around, you were going to hire your own lawyer. But I should have *known* you were going to chicken out."

"You don't understand, Ida. I was getting ready to tell him, but then I saw his old pewter cup on the desk, the one he was given in law school for doing volunteer work for the ACLU, and I suddenly remembered how sensitive he is. Don't you remember how he was going to become a great civil rights lawyer before he decided to become a divorce lawyer instead? It would kill him if I went behind his back and got a second opinion. Separation agreements are his specialty."

"For crying out loud! This is not your obstetrician we're talking about here. This is the coward who ran out on you and Jimmy when the going got rough. Oh, Lord. I can hear you right now. After giving me your solemn promise you'd stand up to him, you stood there wringing your hands—"

"I was sitting."

"—and playing little Miss Prissy. 'Oh, Peter! You're so wise, Peter! Whatever you think is best, Peter!' Honestly, Margaret. Sometimes you act like you haven't got a brain. You didn't sign anything, did you? Because I've told you a thousand times, you don't have to sign anything until you've had a chance to let somebody like Arnold advise you about it."

I looked over at the bottle of rum on the counter, out of reach of the telephone cord, and sighed. I should have known Ida wouldn't understand.

"Margaret?" she asked in her disapproving Tinkerbell voice. "Are you telling me you actually went and signed something?"

"Listen—"

"What?"

"You're wrong about Peter. He didn't try to convince me of anything, Ida. He was extremely kind. He said he wanted to be absolutely fair."

"Hah."

"He's going to let Jimmy and me stay in the house, and I think he's planning on giving us half of his salary."

"You *think*? What's that supposed to mean? You don't even know how much Peter makes, you don't have the first clue about Peter's finances. What gives you the idea he'd tell you the truth? He's had you on an allowance ever since you got married. You think that's because he's generous? He doesn't *want* you to know anything about his finances."

I stretched the telephone cord as far as I could and then swung my left leg up on the counter and tried to nudge the bottle toward me with my foot. Ida was being totally mean about Peter. She was almost the only friend I knew who wasn't on an allowance.

"Besides," I said, as the bottle tipped over and rolled away from my foot, "this isn't like a divorce. It's just a trial separation. And I know Peter better than you do. He's going to wake up one morning and feel terrible about what he's done. But until he feels that terrible, I can't take a chance by doing anything that would make him mad at me."

"Uh-huh. Well, let me break the news to you, Margaret. This

isn't one of Annie D.'s soap operas; this is your *life*. And you better stop sitting around feeling sorry for yourself, expecting Peter to do everything for you. You better start doing something for yourself. You're entitled by law to half of everything Peter owns. Everything he's probably hiding from you right this minute. If you don't get busy protecting your own interests, you and Jimmy are going to find yourselves out on the streets. Trust me. Peter is a lawyer, and he knows all the tricks."

I didn't answer. The trouble with Ida was she thought my husband was like hers. But Peter wasn't at all like Arnold, who was always thinking up ways to make more money. The thing I'd always loved most about Peter was his idealism.

"He's extremely ethical," I reminded Ida.

"Extremely in control," she shot back. "Extremely into an affair with a girl young enough to be his daughter."

I suddenly felt weak and trembly, as though somebody had drained my blood while I wasn't looking. After I finished talking to Ida, I was going to fix myself another drink, go upstairs and ask Jimmy about his final exams, and then I was going to take a long hot bath.

"Oh, good grief," I heard Ida groaning. "I should have guessed. You didn't even read the agreement before you signed it, did you?"

Yes. I was going to sink into a hot tub of bubbles, let the water burn away a layer at a time . . .

"Margaret? Are you listening?"

Yes, I was listening. But I was also suddenly remembering why I'd felt so sorry for Peter when I was in his office. It was because of the pencils he kept in the pewter cup. They were different from the last time I'd seen them. Now they were covered all over with teeth marks.

"He's going to screw you," I heard Ida saying just before I hung up on her. "If you don't start fighting back, that son of a bitch is going to screw you *good*."

———

The noise from Jimmy's stereo greeted me as I walked up the stairs. *I'll break away! I'll leave today!*

I found my son sitting cross-legged on the floor of his bedroom, polishing his military boots. I leaned down and handed him Annie D.'s note.

"Murder," I said. "What on earth do you think she meant? Has another child been found?"

Jimmy glanced at it without getting up. "That's a 'd,' Mom. 'M-u-d-d-e-r.' You're supposed to call Grandmother back."

"Oh," I said, keeping my voice casual. "Your grandmother's probably worried about me."

When he didn't respond, I reached behind him, turned down the volume on his stereo, and added: "I don't think she liked the idea of my having to go downtown by myself."

Jimmy is his father's son: narrow shoulders, dark eyes that look up at you from an angle.

"Yeah?" he said. "So, did you see Dad?"

"Yes. He seems remarkably hale and hearty. I think he's joined a tanning parlor."

Jimmy grinned. He unfolded his legs, pulled himself from the floor, and went over to his desk. He has his father's walk. Easy. Relaxed. All the time in the world to get where he's going. He stood with his back to me. "Well? Is he still mad at you?" His father's detached tone of voice: deep, quiet. A voice that knows what it knows.

"Don't be stupid," I said. "Your father's not mad at me."

Jimmy shrugged.

"Listen! Did he tell you he was mad at me?"

No answer. Jimmy is not his father's son for nothing. He knows how to play the game his dad learned from his own father before him: never tell the mother anything, protect her from the truth.

"So, Dad's coming back home?" he finally asked.

"He's considering it. He's giving it his most serious consideration."

"That's great, Mom." He picked up a stack of photographs

lying on top of his desk and slipped them inside a drawer before I had a chance to see them. "I told you not to worry. I told you everything would work out okay between you two." He sat down on the edge of his bed and began testing the spin on one of the spurs attached to his boots.

I sank down on the other bed, determined not to show my anger at him. As I sipped my Muddy Waters, I contemplated the thought that what annoys a father about his son is not always the same thing that annoys a mother. It wasn't Jimmy's army surplus uniforms or the belt he wore around his waist to hold fake bullets that nagged my heart. Or the way he'd shaved one side of his head and dyed the other side orange and purple. I was even getting used to the idea that he'd stuck a needle through his right earlobe so he could hang a hatchet earring there. No! What was killing my soul at the moment was Jimmy's lousy attitude: he was so damned cheerful.

"Jimmy," I said. "Remember when you were eleven and I drove you home from that Little League game your team lost 28 to 4? Remember how you told me the worst part of losing was not the lopsided score but the fact that you had to listen to your mother telling you what a great game you pitched and how everything was going to be terrific the next time out? If you were so smart at eleven, why can't you be that smart at sixteen?"

He answered by flopping backward on the bed and wrinkling the clothes I'd laid out for him. We were going to celebrate the beginning of his spring break and the end of his exams by having dinner somewhere together.

"Well, never mind," I said, regretting my little story about the game. "How *were* your exams, darling?"

"No sweat," he answered, without raising his head. "I told you there wasn't any point in cramming all night."

I made no comment. He used to compete against his sister for high grades. Even after she died, he'd made the Honor Roll. But after this school year began, he'd lost interest. When he got his papers back, whatever the problem was, it was not his responsibility. Someone had stolen his textbook. Somebody had misplaced his notes. The teacher was lousy. Instead of studying for his exams, he had spent his evenings in the basement developing photographs.

I looked over at him and stifled a sigh. Jimmy liked everything about Arcadia Heights—the swimming pools, the tennis courts, the fact that our house was only a mile from the Chattahoochee River—but what he liked best was the darkroom his father had built for him in the basement. On nights and weekends he spent hours alone down there. Sometimes, when he was at school, I would unlock the door, turn on the light, and stare at the latest pictures he'd hung from a string to dry. I didn't understand what he thought he was supposed to be doing. What I did understand, I didn't like.

The photographs he used to take were of people and objects I knew: the basketball net attached to our old garage, the family playing Scrabble on the porch of the cabin at Lake Burton. Jimmy's new pictures made me uneasy. I didn't approve of the attachment he'd bought for his Nikon that allowed him to sneak up on people, capturing them unawares. I'd seen the way he would stand with his camera aimed at a tree or a cat, pretending to be interested in form or movement, while secretly his lens would be pointed at someone like Dr. Weathers, the retired pediatrician whose nurse pushes him down the sidewalk every afternoon in a wheelchair, or at the Marchesons' little girl that time we saw her squatting on the curb of Demeter Drive, poking a stick at a dead squirrel.

One morning when I went into the darkroom to find the pictures he'd taken of Harold and me while we were planting the azaleas, I discovered he had actually been clicking his shutter at poor old Mrs. Ferguson, our next-door neighbor. There was something cruel about the way Jimmy had caught her stooping half-blind over her rosebushes, crushing aphids between her fingers.

"Well," I said, pulling myself off the bed, "if you're not going to tell me anything about your exams, I guess I'll let you get back to whatever you were doing."

"I told you. They went great, Mom."

Jimmy folded his hands under his head and began whistling through his teeth.

I paused at the door. "So, where do you want to eat? Since you're the honored guest, you get to choose."

Jimmy stared at the ceiling and began naming places he knew I hated: El Mexicano, Barbarella's Pizza, the China Platter, the Western Ranch House.

"Ah, well," I said. "Fortunately, I made reservations at the club, just in case."

"Aw, Mom!" he howled, finally raising his head to look at me. "That's the stuffiest place in town."

"And stop lying on your good gray suit. You're going to ruin it."

"All we'll see are a lot of old ladies sitting around counting their chins."

"Did you hear me, Jimmy? Get your fanny off the bed and hang up your suit."

He rolled over on his side and turned up the volume on his stereo. *I'll break away! I'll leave today!*

"And watch the time!" I shouted over the noise. "We've got to be there at seven sharp."

I shut the door behind me and headed back downstairs to the kitchen to fix another drink and get the separation agreement I'd left on the counter. I didn't want to be like my son. Before I returned my mother's telephone call, I needed to read it so that I could answer everything she had a right to know.

———

"How are you doing?" my mother asks me almost every day.

"Fine," I answer. "And you?"

"Oh, Margaret," she asks: "How are you *doing*, dear?"

This conversation never happens out loud, of course. Out loud, we don't mention Meg's death or the fact that Peter has left Jimmy

and me stranded in the suburbs. We say nothing at all about
Daddy's stroke which has left him half-paralyzed and unable to
speak. Instead, when Mother and I talk over the phone or when I
drop by her house once a week, we play it safe with comfortable
complaints.

"Ah, well," she says, sitting across from me at her breakfast
room table, "what can one do? I've been going to Betty forever,
but no matter how often I tell her, she continues to cut my hair
too short on the sides."

"Ah, well," I sigh in return, pretending not to hear the nurse
in the den talking in a loud singsong voice to Daddy as though he
were a child, "I should never have let that saleslady persuade me
to buy this dress. It makes me look too thin, don't you think?"

Mother is almost as tall as I am. We have the same deep-set
blue eyes, the same narrow mouth and lightly freckled skin. We
sometimes share a nervous gesture of brushing imaginary strands
of hair from our foreheads.

"Never mind," she murmurs, dropping her hand to her lap.
"My friends are too kind to say anything to my face about the
fabric that idiotic decorator put on my living room sofa . . ."

In the silence that follows, we sip our coffee. We press our thin
lips against our china cups to keep from screaming.

"Well," I say after a while, "I guess it's time I went. I'll just run
in and tell Daddy good-bye."

"Now, let her go, Walter," she'll say cheerily, following me into
the den a few minutes later. "I'm sure Margaret has better things
to do than waste all morning with us."

At the front door she twists her diamond wedding band around
and around on her finger. We avoid each other's eyes.

As I head down the front walk to the car, I hear her sighing behind my back. "Oh," she sighs, unable to pretend any longer that
she has not noticed all the unpleasant things that are happening
to everyone she loves. "Oh . . ."

The separation agreement was hidden inside a large envelope. Instead of writing my name on the outside of it, Miss Grimsley had pencilled "Hers."

I brought it upstairs with me, and while I waited for the tub to fill, I lay down on the chaise lounge beside the phone and prepared to read what I had signed.

My initial thought after I opened the envelope and scanned a couple of pages was that Peter had already lost a few brain cells at the relatively young age of forty-six. His wording was total gobbledegook: *party of the first part, party of the second.* I flipped through the rest of the pages until I finally found my name in the Addendum.

PERSONAL LIVING EXPENSES

INCURRED BY

MRS. PETER SCOTT BRIDGES JUNIOR

Beneath this was a column listing every check I'd written over the past year.

On the next page was a shorter column: PAYMENTS TO BE MADE TO MARGARET HUNTER BRIDGES.

I stared at the arithmetic on the last page. Here was the sum total of Peter's version of an ethical lawyer's financial obligations to his wife and child. The bottom line informed me that unless I managed to get a job paying $53,792.17, I would end up a bag lady.

The phone was ringing. I drained my glass and peeped at the final paragraph. Eighteen words. Eighteen words in capital letters that concisely expressed what my husband had been trying to tell me he needed: IF THE PARTY OF THE SECOND PART AGREES TO AN UNCONTESTED DIVORCE, THE ABOVE TERMS MAY BE RENEGOTIATED.

I glanced over to where the bubbles from the tub were beginning to inch their way onto the bedroom rug.

"Mom?" I heard Jimmy calling. "The phone's for *you!*"

"Renegotiated," I murmured. I realized I had probably never

heard that word actually said aloud by anybody before in my whole entire life.

"*Re*-ne-go-ti-a-ted" . . . "Re-ne-*go*-ti-a-ted . . ."

"It's Grandmother," Jimmy announced, poking his head through the door. "And don't talk all night. The club gets ticked off as hell if you're late for dinner reservations."

"*Re*-ne-go-ti-a-ted," I amended, straightening the papers and hiding them back inside the envelope. "Have you ever heard that word before, darling?"

"Jesus!" he said. "You forgot to turn off the water!" He raced into the bathroom and began slinging towels on the floor. "You almost flooded the place!" he howled in his father's voice. Critical. Accusing.

JimmyJimmyJimmy. Always finding fault with his mother . . .

"Aw, *Mom*," he said, pressing a towel on the bedroom rug to absorb the bubbles. "Are you just going to sit there and watch?"

No. I was going to run downstairs and get a mop so I could help my son clean up the mess. And while I was downstairs, I was going to pick up the phone and talk to my mother.

———

"Mother? Is this a good time?" I said.

"Yes. It's a very good time. I was just this minute getting ready to phone you again."

I waited for her to express her anxiety about my meeting with Peter. Instead, she began talking about a friend of mine—she couldn't remember the name, but it was the one who had gotten a divorce a few years back and Peter had handled the arrangements.

"Your father and I have been thinking about that poor girl all day long," Mother said. "How much did he give her?"

"How much did who give *whom*?"

"Her ex-husband. The one who ran away with the daughter of his business partner. Your father and I wanted to know if she got a fair settlement."

I had no idea. I wondered if Mother would be just as happy learning the terms of my settlement.

"Margaret? Are you still there?"

Yes. I was still there. But it's not all that easy lying to your mother, even when you know that truth will kill a mother quicker than anything on earth.

"Well, Margaret?"

"Actually, Mother, I don't know the details of that particular divorce. I'm sorry. I do know that in the case of Peter and myself, he is taking care of everything."

"Yes?"

"House notes," I lied. "Insurance. Utilities. Medical expenses. All tuition and books for Jimmy."

"Food and clothing, I should hope."

"Also food and clothing."

"What about your weekly allowance, Margaret? Is he keeping that up?"

"Yes."

"And the house at Lake Burton?"

"We have generous visitation rights."

"That's all down in writing? You have that written down some-where?"

"Yes. In neat columns."

Mother hesitated. I could see her in my mind's eye. She'd be sitting on the Sheraton sofa in the living room, brushing an imaginary strand of hair from her forehead. "Well, that's good," she finally said. "And I imagine Peter has taken care of Harold and Annie D.?"

Harold and Annie D.! They were like family. Annie D. had been with us for at least three years, ever since Peter took a pro-bono case and got her off on probation by promising the judge he would find her an honest job. But Harold! He had been with us since before Meg and Jimmy were in nursery school. And now Peter was going to force me to throw them out on the streets with his son and me.

"What did you say, dear?"

"I said yes. Annie D., and Harold, too. Believe me, Mother, Peter has thought of every detail. Separation agreements are his specialty. He hasn't missed a trick."

"Well, that's quite generous of Peter . . ."

I waited for the magic word.

"But . . ."

"Yes, Mother?"

"I'm afraid your father and I will never be able to quite forgive him for what he's doing to you and Jimmy and the rest of the family. We've always loved Peter. We just wonder if there could be something the matter with him, Margaret."

"Listen," I said. "I'm sorry, but now that you mention it, this is actually not all that good a time for me to talk, Mother. I'm taking Jimmy out to dinner tonight, and—"

"Your father wanted me to ask if you thought poor Peter might need—"

"—you know how annoyed the club gets when you're late."

"—a bit of . . . (whisper) . . . *psychological help*."

4

It took me longer than I'd expected to get off the telephone with Mother and take a bath and find something suitable to wear. Jimmy was waiting for me in the garage, slumped behind the steering wheel of the new Spitfire his father had given him as a going-away present. I said, "I'm sorry, darling. But never mind. We'll make it on time."

Jimmy frowned and backed out of the garage without a word.

"And you look like such a gentleman in that suit, Jimmy!"

As we screeched down the driveway in reverse, I saw his hatchet earring swinging dangerously close to his shaved scalp and I reached over to stop the motion.

"Aw, *Mom*," he said in his disapproving voice. He gunned the motor through the intersection of Hercules and Demeter and roared out of the gates of Arcadia Heights onto the access road leading to the expressway. "Admit it," he said. "The Carriage Country Club is the dullest place in Atlanta."

No. I lay my head against the backrest of my little bucket seat. I closed my eyes so I wouldn't see him tearing off the expressway ramp into traffic. The Carriage Country Club wasn't the most boring place in Atlanta, I wanted to tell him. Your mother has always *loved* the Carriage Country Club.

The Carriage Country Club was founded in 1881 by Jimmy's

great-great-great grandfather along with two hundred of his friends. According to the original charter, their purpose was "to provide a refuge for our wives and children, where they might be protected from Improper Characters."

Despite what Meg used to think, and Jimmy probably still does, the term "Improper Characters" has never meant anything racial. One hundred years ago it referred to the white carpetbaggers who had come South to turn the ashes of a little railroad boomtown into a city bursting with what my Grandmother Leticia called "Yankee Dudes." ("Dear heart!" she'd say. "Strutters and flaunters! They may have attempted to ape the customs of southern breeding, but they made a total mockery of it in the process. Why, your great-grandmother told me they wore hair pomade! Leather and prunella shoes!")

In 1981 the term remains nonracial, although it may be true that no Jews or blacks or Orientals belong to the Carriage Country Club. No recent Hispanics. Or women, of course. The Carriage Country Club remains most definitely a gentleman's club, but they are the kind of gentlemen who remain gracious about extending guest privileges to their wives and children.

Yes. I've always loved the club. My childhood memories include Easter egg hunts on the golf course and Fourth of July fireworks across the lake. Labor Days chasing goldfish in the baby pool. Christmas Eves with Santa in the Poinsettia Parlor.

My high school scrapbook is still crammed with crushed corsages from Calvin Academy dances where I flounced my hoopskirts to "Tutti Frutti!" in the same ballroom in which two years later I would be presented to society on the arm of my father, and in which only three months after that I would wear my grandmother's wedding dress and dance with Peter to "Jailhouse Rock."

Peter. Tall and dark and handsome Peter. The kind of boy who spoke in a slow, sensual voice that encouraged a girl to stop pretending to laugh at her date's joke about a black on a Freedom Ride through Alabama and turn instead to her best friend's date who was discussing the Berlin Wall, the Cuban Missile Crisis, the symbolism of his favorite poet, T. S. Eliot.

"You can't be serious," Ida said the night I confessed I might be falling in love with a law student from Emory. "Peter's so *boring*."

It was July. Ida and I were renting a cottage at Sea Island after our sophomore year at Sweet Briar.

That afternoon we'd made plans to have a hot-dog roast on the beach with some of the other college students we'd met around The Cloister swimming pool. While the girls spread blankets on the sand and set out the potato salad and baked beans and paper plates and bug spray provided by the staff, the boys stood around making a huge bonfire from the driftwood and seaweed that the girls had gathered earlier while the boys played volleyball.

My date for the party was a Phi Delta Theta from the University of North Carolina. His name was Arnold Matthews. Arnold, it turned out, was a boy who enjoyed automotive engines. He had the ability to describe something called a carburetor for a half an hour without once shifting to another subject.

My best friend missed this educational experience because she and her date didn't show up until almost seven-thirty. The rest of us had already settled down on our blankets to eat.

"Peter Bridges," she announced, introducing Arnold and me to a boy who had a band of white skin showing just above his low-riding bathing suit.

"Hi," I said. I noticed his thick neck, small ears, narrow shoulders.

He nodded. He stood over us, casually tucking his thumbs inside the waist of his bathing suit. I could tell by the way he ignored me that he wasn't all that interested in a tall, thin, redheaded girl named Margaret Hunter, the kind of girl who covered her nose with her hands so nobody would notice she was wearing Noxema.

Ida shot me a glance over Peter's head—*Yes! He's even more boring than he looks!*—and then walked over to the bonfire to roast a couple of hot dogs for him.

He eased himself down beside me on the blanket just as

Arnold was finally moving on to another subject, something called "breaking ninety."

"So far," Arnold said, leaning forward so he could talk to Peter without my being in the way, "the best I've shot is eighty-six."

Peter nodded. "Not bad," he said.

The sun was setting. A deep orange spilled over the horizon and spread across the water.

"That was on the course at High Hampton in North Carolina," Arnold said. "Ever been there yourself?"

"Huh-uh."

I had no special interest in this date of Ida's sitting next to me on the blanket, but while Arnold talked I couldn't help noticing the way Peter's legs were covered with dark hair that traveled up his thighs, disappeared under his bathing suit, and reappeared on the band of white skin. His belly button, I couldn't help seeing, was deep enough to hold a quarter-teaspoon of sand. He had a scar the size of a fraternity pin above his left nipple. A dent in his chin. Full lips. Pug nose. The kind of long black eyelashes some girls would kill for.

It was dark by the time Ida pulled Arnold up from the blanket to join her and the others for skinny-dipping in the waves. She acted as though Peter wasn't even there.

"Come on, Margaret," she said, trying to convince me to actually go behind a sand dune, take off all my clothes, and expose myself to strangers. "Don't be such a prude."

But to tell the truth, I *was* a bit of a prude. Hadn't I lived all my life by my mother's copy of *Mrs. Dull's Guide to Southern Etiquette*? There had not been one single word in that book about the proper way to behave while naked in mixed company. And although I was twenty and past my salad days as a Buckhead pink who flirted with Buckhead jels in the backseats of their fathers' Cadillacs before taking offense at their advances and hugging the car door while explaining, "I'm not that kind of girl," I remained loyal to the Buckhead pink motto: "No sex below the collarbone."

Yes. I was still enough of a pink to know that if I took off my clothes and skinny-dipped in the waves, even in the dark, everybody would discover how swaybacked I was and how my hips were overly large for my body.

As soon as Arnold and Ida left, Peter and I began talking about the sorts of things people our age always discussed: favorite books he had read, the launching of *Sputnik*, the practicality of my bouffant hairdo. The bonfire was low. There was no moon, only stars. Shrimp-boat lights bobbed in the distance.

After a while Peter lay back on the blanket, cushioned his head on his folded arms, and pretended to fall asleep. I sat up, my chin buried in my knees, and listened to the slap of the waves and the occasional *pop!* of the settling fire. The shrill voices of the skinny-dippers seemed far away. Disembodied.

"Margaret," I suddenly heard Peter saying. His voice was a rough whisper. "Come here."

When he reached for me and pulled me down beside him on the blanket, his warm breath on the back of my neck made my hairs quiver. His legs gripped my legs. In the dark it was impossible to see his scar or the dent in his chin. I felt his long eyelashes brushing my cheek. His finger began tracing the line of my spine.

"Listen," I said, pulling away from him to catch my breath. "I've never read James Joyce. You say you find his writing extremely thought-provoking?"

But Peter had apparently said all he wanted to say on the subject of his favorite books. While I tried to think of another subject of mutual interest, his tongue began exploring the curves of my right ear.

"Wait," I said. I leaned across the blanket and began searching through my beach bag for my pack of Pall Malls: a Buckhead pink's best friend. I knew a cigarette was the kind of ladylike defense a girl could always use without hurting the feelings of a boy who had discovered something on hand more stimulating than *Ulysses*.

While I held the lighted cigarette between us like a torch, Peter opened a can of beer and began telling me the kinds of intimate details about himself that a boy only tells a girl when he's planning on making a move. The kinds of intimate dreams, ambitions, disappointments, and heartaches a boy mentions once in his life to a girl and then for the next twenty-three years never mentions or remembers again.

He was twenty-four. A Phi Beta Kappa graduate of the University of Virginia, in his first year at Emory Law School. He had grown up in Richmond, the only child of a Presbyterian minister. He was planning on leading quite a different life from that of his poor parents. His poor parents, he said as he reached over and began retracing the line of my spine with his finger, believed in the virtues of the hereafter; he believed in the virtues of the here and now.

"Oh, Peter!" I said. "I feel just exactly the same way, Peter!"

And his poor parents had never done a single exciting thing in all their lives. Practically the farthest away from Richmond they ever traveled was when they came to Atlanta to visit him.

"I've gotten to the point where I dread to go home, Margaret," he confided, lightly kissing my ear. "Even for weekends. It's so goddamned sad. Like, there's this picture of Mama and Daddy in a silver frame on the mantel. They're standing side by side, they're young, and you can look in their eyes and tell they think they've got the whole world ahead of them. They're just waiting for the day when they'll make their marks." He began blowing softly on the back of my neck. "You know what I mean?" he murmured.

"Oh, yes, Peter!"

"And then I turn around and see Daddy sacked out on the sofa with a newspaper over his face and Mama sitting at the card table working a jigsaw puzzle, and all I can think about is how old they've become. All they do is get up every morning and eat the same brand of cereal and drink the same brand of coffee before they go off to the same sermons and baptisms and weddings and funerals they've gone to all their lives. The same visits to people's houses after church on Sundays to the same dishes of chicken and rice, the same blessings for lost souls, the same announcements over vanilla ice cream: how much money was collected that day in the offering plates, which deacons did the counting."

Peter leaned away from me and opened another can of beer. "I can't stand to look at that photograph of them on the mantel anymore, Margaret," he said mournfully. "Christ, it's depressing . . ."

"*Extremely* depressing," I agreed, sighing. I looked out into the darkness and tried to imagine Peter's parents standing side by side in front of a church. They were probably in their forties now, but in that picture . . . so young! They stared into the camera with farsighted eyes. Their fingers marked the pages in their Bibles where the hope for the new day might be found.

"Ah, Margaret," Peter said wearily. And then he explained how he was going to do something meaningful with his life. He wasn't like his classmates at Emory who planned to become part of the establishment of well-heeled lawyers in well-heeled law firms. He was going to use his knowledge of the law to aid the poor, the black, the uneducated. He wasn't going to end up like his father, a man whose gifts to others were merely words. No. He was going to be a man of action. And he would never allow his wife to end up like his mother, a woman whose goals were tangled up in knots of ladies' Bible classes and church suppers. "A slave to the rigid rules of clergymen's helpmates," he said.

I inhaled the last drag of my cigarette.

"Jesus," Peter murmured. He took the Pall Mall from me and extinguished it in the sand. "Is it too much to ask?" he said, cradling my head on his chest. "To make our lives add up to something important?"

The night was black. The fire was low. The lights from the shrimp boats still bobbed in the distance. And this boy with his legs wrapped around my legs had warm breath that smelled of mustard and hot dogs and noble intentions.

"Tall, dark, and handsome?" Ida asked after we returned to our beach cottage and I told her I might be falling in love with this Peter Bridges boy who had been secretary of the SAE fraternity at the University of Virginia and who had won a scholarship to the Emory University School of Law because of his brilliance as a student of English literature. "You must be kidding," Ida said. "You can't sit there and tell me with a straight face that you think Peter is tall. He's a foot shorter than you are!"

"A couple of inches, Ida. But he's dark and handsome, don't you think?"

"How can you call him dark? He doesn't even have a decent tan."

But he had dark hair. And the band of skin just above his low-riding bathing suit had been white and vulnerable and soft.

"He has black curly hair, Ida," I said. "Relatively speaking, Peter is a rather dark person."

"And you honestly found him handsome? Are you blind? His ears are squashed against his head. He has a pig nose. He has a dent in his chin!"

"A dimple, Ida. Like Cary Grant."

Yes. Peter had a dimple in his chin like my favorite actor. His face was sophisticated.

"I admit Peter Bridges may not be handsome in a movie-star way," I said, frowning at Ida's perverseness, "but when you look at him, don't you see a man brimming with character?"

"Besides which, Margaret," Ida said, ignoring my question, "he must be the most boring boy I've ever met."

"Boring?" I let my mouth hang open so she could see my amazement.

"Oh, come off of it!" With her back to me, Ida sneered into the dressing table mirror. "All he could talk about was books and politics. And he was *my* date, by the way. You totally monopolized him. 'Oh, Peter!' you kept saying. 'That's just exactly the way I feel about it, too, Peter!'" Ida gave her hair one final brushing and began applying cold cream to her face. "And since when, I'd like to know, did Margaret Hunter decide she's always *yearned* to join the Peace Corps?"

I didn't answer. There was no talking to Ida. She had never had a date stolen out from under her before. How could I explain to my best friend how much deeper Peter's mind was than other boys' minds? How much more sincere his dreams and ambitions, his disappointments and heartaches made him than those Buck-head boys I'd dated during those other summers, a million years ago, when I'd been too naive and shallow and prudish to understand that what I needed was to marry a boy whose motives in life were the sex urge and the desire to be great?

"And those depressing people he talks about!" Ida was saying, flicking the elastic to her shortie pajamas and climbing into the other twin bed. "I can't imagine what you think you'd find in common with people like that. Since when did you decide you wanted to become best friends with people who live inside cardboard boxes in vacant lots? Or colored people—I thought I'd die! Can you believe the way Peter actually said right out loud that he admired that nigra boy who urinated on the floor of the downtown Lane Rexall Drugstore when they wouldn't let him use the Whites Only bathroom? I swear to goodness! Peter Bridges may be the very first Communist we've ever met in our whole entire lives!"

Ida settled her head on the pillow in a way that would not disturb her chin strap. She was guarding against ending up like her mother, with a neck that hung down like a turkey's.

"And books," she added sleepily. "That boy knows the plots and characters of every book he's ever read . . ."

Yes. Peter knew his books. "You remind me of Holden Caulfield's girlfriend playing checkers," he'd told me. "Always on the defensive. Always keeping her kings on the back row." He'd reached over and grabbed my cigarette out of my mouth. He'd stubbed it out in the sand. "Come here, Margaret," he'd said then, pulling me down on his chest.

"Well, never you mind," Ida was saying from the bed next to mine. "It doesn't matter. Peter's leaving tomorrow to spend the rest of the summer with his parents in Richmond. You'll never have to be bored by him again."

I looked over at her. "He told you that? He's leaving for the whole summer?"

She turned on her side and switched off the bedside lamp. "Go to sleep, Margaret. I'm exhausted."

But I knew I would never be able to sleep now. Why had I made such a fool of myself? Oh! If only I'd jumped up from the blanket when the others decided to go skinny-dipping. If only I'd had enough sense to run behind a sand dune, strip off my bathing suit, and swim naked with those strangers.

But suddenly it had been too late. They were already down by the water. The stars were above us—no moon—and one minute a boy I hardly knew was sitting beside me calmly discussing *The Catcher in the Rye* and the next minute he was . . .

Our Father who art in Heaven, Hallowed be Thy . . .

Oh, my God. The next minute he was feeling me up!

Yes. His fingers were slipping under the straps of my bathing suit, uh-huh. His palms were . . . *Forgive us our debts, as we forgive our debtors!*

And it seemed like no time at all before I heard Ida and Arnold and the others returning. The fire was low now, crackling softly. And the others began singing songs from a thousand summers ago without the least idea that on the other side of that low, crackling fire . . .

His legs were gripping my legs.

"You are my sunshine . . . ," they were singing. "Down by the old mill stream . . ."

His finger was reaching inside the crotch of my bathing suit.

"I love you, Peter," I whispered.

And I love God the Father, God the Son, and God the Holy Ghost. And I believe in all things visible and invisible and once, when I was a little girl, I slept in a big four-poster bed so high I used to climb up on a box to reach it so my mother could hear my prayers, so my daddy could hear my prayers, so later . . . when I was almost twelve . . . my Grandmother Leticia in Heaven could hear my . . . ("Never touch yourself down there!" she'd warned me. "You'll go blind, Margaret!")

And then they started singing songs from the Hit Parade: "That'll Be the Day" . . . "Kisses Sweeter Than Wine" . . . "I Believe" . . .

"Yes," I whispered to Peter while his fingers reached to find me. " 'I believe for every drop of rain that falls, a flower grows . . .' "

"Shhh . . ."

" 'And I believe that even in the darkest night, a candle glows.' "

"Don't talk, Margaret . . ."

Yes. Stop talking. Boys don't like girls to talk when they're trying to concentrate on . . .

"Ah," he said, his finger reaching the wetness he'd been needing to reach ever since he'd stood over me and heard my name for the first time and tucked his thumbs inside the waist of his low-riding suit. "I think I love you, too, Margaret."

Oh, my God. Dear God . . .

"Thy kingdom come, Thy will be done," I prayed silently in bed after Ida had turned off the light. And while I prayed I listened to the waves breaking on the other side of the window, far down the beach, and I thought of my Grandmother Leticia, who would have ended up in the poorhouse if she hadn't done away with herself instead.

Peter was leaving the next morning. Why hadn't he said a word to me about it? He was going away. I'd never see him again. How could I have been so dumb? Why hadn't I realized Peter was just like every other boy my grandmother had warned me about when I was too young to understand the warning?

I should have known he could never love a shallow Buckhead pink like me. A boy with his mind, a boy who was so idealistic he planned to dedicate his life to poor people could never be interested in a fluffy-headed girl who was so stupid she came right out and admitted she'd never read *Ulysses*. A girl so immature she wondered out loud—to a boy who had won a scholarship for knowing all there was to know about literature!—if it had ever crossed his mind that Henry James wrote like a fairy.

"Ida!" I cried, getting out of my bed and shaking her awake. "I've done something terrible!"

Ida opened her eyes. Turned on the light. Watched me squatting on the floor between the beds, hugging myself and crying.

"What on earth have you gone and done *now*?" she asked in her annoyed Tinkerbell voice. "What in the world is the matter?"

But there was no talking to Ida. There was no telling her that

I'd gone and done what she and Joyce Belinda and Mary Earle and I and all the rest of our Buckhead pink crowd had solemnly sworn we would never do until we got married. And now it was hopeless. I'd become a lapsed virgin. And maybe it was worse than that! Maybe I was a *non*-virgin! Maybe a finger counted as much as the real thing! Maybe if it was a finger belonging to the son of a Presbyterian minister, a finger belonging to the first boy I'd ever met in my life who was born and raised in the South and still admitted out loud he was an agnostic, it counted the same as a penis!

Oh, Peter. He was the only person, boy or girl, I'd ever known with the courage to admit out loud what I'd tried so hard not to admit even to myself. That despite memorizing the Children's Catechism to join the Buckhead Presbyterian Church when I was twelve—perhaps *because* I'd memorized the Children's Catechism when I was twelve—there was a possibility that I might be an agnostic, too.

"Ah, well," I told Ida. "It's not important. I just feel like killing myself, that's all."

"You know what your trouble is?" Ida said, turning off the light. "You enjoy exaggerating your miseries better than anybody I know. Now go to sleep, for heaven's sake, and stop worrying. You'll never have to see that boy again."

No. But over twenty-three years later, as I rode beside my son to the club where I'd danced in my grandmother's wedding dress to "Hearts Made of Stone," I remembered how I *would* never have to see Peter Bridges again. And I remembered how I'd felt that night so long ago at Sea Island. How sad I'd been when Ida told me he was leaving the next day for Richmond. And how happy I'd been just hours earlier, when I was lying on a blanket with Peter in the dark.

———

"Hah!" Jimmy cried.

I opened my eyes in time to see him roaring through a yellow light and high-fiving the ceiling for luck.

"Don't," I said. I sat up straight and tried to visualize my hips as small enough to fit comfortably inside the little bucket seat. I realized I was beginning to feel dizzy from going around all the curves. "Slow down, son."

"Relax," he said. "We're almost there. In another two minutes you'll be listening to the mellow sounds of old fogies farting."

"Oh, *Jimmy*." When had he begun talking so filthy? "Not fogies," I may or may not have said out loud. "Refined." Because at the Carriage Country Club a lady could arrive at the front entrance and be assisted from her car by a man who would tip his hat and say, "Good evening, Mrs. Bridges. It's a mighty fine evening, isn't it, Mrs. Bridges?"

She could walk—she could *stride*—through the lobby of the club past cages of singing birds.

She could climb the winding staircase—perhaps she would hear Chopin being played by the man at the piano in the Poinsettia Parlor—and as she made her way through the hallway to the dining room she could glance at herself in mirrored walls. How nice you look tonight in your blue cocktail dress, Mrs. Bridges. Doesn't everyone see how nice Mrs. Bridges looks tonight?

Then she could wait with Jimmy at the door into the dining room. Nobody would be rude enough to mention the shaved side of her son's head, the orange and purple on the other side. And in a moment Mike or George or Charles would say: "Good evening, Mrs. Bridges. A table for two this evening, Mrs. Bridges?"

And the waiters would know her other favorite drink: the dry martini. "Tanqueray, Mrs. Bridges? Three olives as usual?"

And they would treat her like a lady without making a big deal about it, because nobody ever made a big deal about it at the Carriage Country Club.

Yes. After a hard day, after a lady has had to sign her past away before she's even had a chance to read it, after a lady has been forced to realize that the man she's been married to for over twenty-three years has just screwed her good, she can simply relax.

Ah, indeed yes, Mrs. Bridges. For a few pleasant hours she could enjoy a Mother's Night Out. Spend a quiet evening telling her son everything she's been needing to tell him since the day he was born.

"I love you, Jimmy," she would say. "I'm proud to claim you as my son."

And then she could explain how none of this estrangement business was his fault. It was nobody's fault. "Not your father's fault," she could lie, "and certainly not your mother's."

She could reach across the table in the dining room of the club and affectionately squeeze his hand before bringing up the little matter that bothered her so much. "Hello, good-bye—that's all you ever say to me. You act as though you find me irrelevant, an unnecessary burden in your life. Damn you, Jimmy! You behave more and more like your father every day. You're going to be sorry, young man."

Yes! "Your mother may not be around here much longer. Your mother may decide she doesn't have to go on living like this," she'll tell him.

No. Never mind. Settle back in the lovely Louis XVI chair and enjoy the lovely view. Run your manicured fingers over the pink linen cloth. Lean down and sniff the roses in the crystal vase. Feel the weight of the silver soup spoon in your hand.

And after the vichyssoise, she will concentrate on her entree, perhaps the Dover sole. Never overcooked. Always perfectly seasoned. Accompanied on the plate by an arrangement of fresh vegetables.

"Beautifully presented," she'll remember to tell the waiter. "Such precious little baby Brussel sprouts!"

"Dessert, Mrs. Bridges?"

"Oh, why not? What do *you* think, Jimmy? The Grand Marnier Soufflé?"

No. If it's available tonight, the famous Carriage Country Cake. Inspired by the visit of President Coolidge or Cleveland or one of those other dead presidents whose last name began with a *C.* The one who visited that time and demonstrated he was overly fond of rum.

Or, on second thought, just coffee. Yes. Another cup of your delicious coffee, thank you. Because Mrs. Bridges is feeling just a wee bit woozy, just a wee bit into her fog.

Certainly, *something* seemed to have happened while she was relaxing in her son's Spitfire with her eyes closed. Because someone was just now opening the car door and helping her crawl out of the little bucket seat. And she was trying to remember something . . .

Had she accidentally fixed herself one too many Muddy Waters? How many Muddy Waters had Mrs. Bridges accidentally fixed?

As her son came up alongside her, she wondered if perhaps she should have listened to her mother after all. Perhaps the Carriage Country Club was not the wisest choice, her mother had suggested over the telephone. But it was too late now. She walked ahead of her son, who considered her irrelevant, and she anticipated what she would say to Mike or Charles or George: "You're looking particularly fine this evening," she'd say. "It's so fine to see you looking so fine."

She remembered she wanted to glance at herself as she passed through the mirrored hallway, but somehow she and Jimmy had already reached the entrance into the dining room and Mike was coming toward them. She waited for him to ask her if she wanted a special table by the window. "Overlooking the rose garden, Mrs. Bridges?"

Except Mike was not asking her anything at all. He was saying, "Please wait here, Mrs. Bridges." And the manager coming up behind him was the manager with the beady eyes, the bald head, the very man—she suddenly understood this so clearly it was as though she were having an epiphany!—that Buford used to tell her about when she was a little girl playing in the woods across the street. Yes! He might very well be the man who'd strangled his wife in the creek bed and dragged her body through the pine forest and tried to stuff her body in the trunk of his car. And when her body had been too tall to stuff, when it had become too stiff to fold, he'd done the only thing a man could do. He'd chopped off her legs with a hatchet and hidden them in the underbrush near the train trestle for a little girl to trip over, Buford had warned her, if she weren't extremely careful to look where she was going.

The manager was standing in front of her now, blocking the entrance into the dining room. He was placing his hand on her arm—Dear God! He was actually touching Mrs. Bridges on the arm!—and he was leading her back toward the mirrored hallway.

"I'm sorry," he was saying in a voice so low she had to bend down to hear it, "but one of our board members—I believe Mr. Willowford is a law partner of Mr. Bridges?—is dining with us this evening, and he has just informed me that you are no longer eligible to enjoy family privileges. This is a gentleman's club, Mrs. Bridges."

Ah, well. A gentleman's club. The manager was so very sorry. And Mrs. Bridges was so very sorry, too.

"Come on, Mom."

Her son was tugging at her sleeve.

"It doesn't matter, Mom. We'd rather eat somewhere better."

Yes! They'd rather eat the worms in the meat sauce of Barbarella's spaghetti. The ground cat—she'd always suspected it—in the chalupas at El Mexicano. The black hairs in the Moo Goo Gai Pan at the China Platter.

"Now, Mrs. Bridges," the man was whispering again. "We don't want to go and make a scene, do we?"

But she *did* want to make a scene! She wanted to go and make a scene extremely much. She wanted to brush this little twit aside and stride into the dining room and tell that old fat Mr. Willowford—he was probably sitting at her favorite table overlooking the rose garden even though everybody in Atlanta knew he made his money defending slumlords and crooked contractors, he ought to be in *prison!*—that the only reason her estranged husband had been able to join this bigoted Good Old Boy's club in the first place was because Mrs. Bridges's great-grandfather, and her grandfather, and her father had *allowed* him to join! "You don't think for one minute he could have gotten into this gentleman's club on his *own*, do you?" she wanted to ask everybody sitting in the dining room eating her Dover sole. "Why, Mr. Bridges is an *agnostic!*"

And she wanted to point her finger at the widow sitting in the corner wearing all the turkey chins. "Does everybody here know old Mrs. Jester?" she wanted to scream. "The so-called lady who's always getting her picture in the paper for giving money to the arts? I'm here to tell you she cheats at bridge and she's the biggest lush in Buckhead!"

Oh, yes. Mrs. Bridges wanted to make these scenes, and she wanted to make many, many other scenes. But, unfortunately, Mrs. Bridges couldn't seem to move.

"Mom?"

Somebody was calling to her from far away.

"Let's go, Mom."

No. She was definitely in her fog. And she wouldn't be able to come out of the fog until she had made the one obligatory scene that needed to be made.

———

"Jesus," Jimmy said when we got home. He steered me through the kitchen to the back stairway. "Why do you always have to act like that? By tomorrow, everybody in Atlanta will be talking about us."

"It wasn't my fault." I leaned against his chest and tried to count the number of steps I'd have to climb in order to reach my bedroom. "That man made me do it, darling."

He pushed me away. "It's embarrassing, Mom."

Yes. My son with the fake bullets and the hatchet earring was ashamed of his mother.

Ah, JimmyJimmyJimmy. What had happened to him? When he was two, he'd worn little sailor pants that buttoned at the crotch. Little white high-topped shoes.

"Oh, Jimmy!" I cried. "I loved those high-topped shoes. I used to polish them for you every day."

"Come on, Mom," he said, gripping me under the armpits and half dragging me toward the living room. "Why don't you just lie down for a while?"

"You used to be such a sensitive child," I said. "Remember? 'I've dug you a hole in the backyard and filled it with water, Mom,' you said when you were five. 'It's the pond you've always needed to read beside.'"

And he used to be such a *gentleman.* Why, in the second grade he even wrote poetry! *Everyone loves my mother I bet / Except those who haven't met her yet.*

"How proud I was, Jimmy, of that Woodsman Badge you earned in the Cub Scouts. Remember? And the Camp Pelican Certificate of Merit in Sailing?"

Somewhere in the attic was a blue Buckhead T-ball jersey with a red 11 on the back of it. And somewhere in a cardboard box, sealed with masking tape for safekeeping, was my son's Peewee basketball uniform. On the floor of his closet were eighth-grade football pads and helmets, tenth-grade soccer shoes, Camp Pelican Junior Counselor T-shirts. A navy blazer with brass buttons exactly like the brass buttons on his father's and his grandfather's navy blazers.

Oh! He used to be his father's son, all right. In khaki pants and tasseled loafers. Dark curly hair.

"Ah, Jimmy." I flopped down on the living room sofa. "I'm sorry, darling. Your mother is just . . . *extremely* . . . sorry . . ."

"Good night, Mom."

"But tell me the truth," I ordered, flinging my arm out to grab the lapel of his lovely gray suit before he could get away. "Didn't you think it was rather repulsive the way that murderer just stood there in front of everybody in the Carriage Country Club and never even bothered to wipe off his face?"

———

"Jesus H. Christ!" Peter howled in my dreams that night. "Why can't you be more like my girlfriend Dr. Roberts? I'll have you know Dr. Roberts has never vomited on anyone in her whole entire life!"

"Don't listen to him," my friend Mary Earle Kennedy said. My friend was making mud pies on the bank of the creek across the street. She had on white gloves so she wouldn't get her hands dirty. "Since God gave me my cancer," she said, "I vomit all the time . . ."

Part Two

"Those dreams were concurrent with the one I was having about a quiz show on television," I call to Harold. "Imagine! I was standing inside an isolation booth about to win a total of $53,792.17!"

"Yes, ma'am," Harold answers from the other side of the chimney. "Jimmy be back at your window again."

I don't interrupt my story by looking. There is every possibility my son does not approve of what he's seeing through the telescopic lens of his camera. He's probably the only boy at Calvin Academy whose mother is sitting on the roof of a house with her yardman.

"I couldn't remember the question I was supposed to answer, but I wasn't worried. I knew the show was rigged, and as soon as I got my money I was planning to snitch to the newspapers that the reason contestants always looked up at the ceiling of the booth was because that was where the master of ceremonies taped the correct response."

"Uh-huh. That's the truth, Miz Margaret."

Tick. Silence. *Tock-tock.*

The clock on the wall was driving me crazy. It kept skipping beats. I was the only one who seemed to realize it was totally out of sync with the natural rhythms of the world.

"And now, Mrs. Bridges," I suddenly heard the master of ceremonies saying, "time has run out. I must have your answer immediately."

I winked at him. In another second or two, the $53,792.17 would be mine.

"Yes, Mrs. Bridges?"

I raised my eyes to the ceiling.

"Time's up," he said.

I turned toward him and tapped on the glass. "Excuse me," I whispered. "I'm afraid someone has made a dreadful mistake. The answer on the piece of paper is illegible, it's nothing but scrawls."

"Too bad," he said. He faced the studio audience. "Now, isn't that too bad?"

"Wait!" I screamed. "It wasn't my fault, you nincompoop! Somebody's gone and rigged it unfairly."

The sound of my voice woke me up. "Mom?" I heard Jimmy calling to me from upstairs.

"Never mind," I mumbled. I grabbed the sofa pillow and crammed it under my head so that I could return to the dream. But I was no longer inside the isolation booth. I was striding across the stage toward the master of ceremonies!

"And you know what he said to me, Harold? 'Sorry,' he said. He stood in front of the booth, barring the door, and said, 'This is a gentleman's dream. I'm afraid you're no longer eligible to participate.'"

I listen for Harold's chuckle, but I get only silence. I am not surprised. He hasn't had much to say since I started describing everything that happened last night. Nor has our hostess.

It has been almost an hour since Ida stopped screaming at us from the patio. A few minutes ago she came out of the house dressed in her new Fila tennis outfit. At this very moment she and Joyce Belinda Johnson and two other members of our Buckhead Bombers team are over at the recreation center waging unholy battle against the newly formed Arcadia Heights Harpies in the C-level finals of the Atlanta Lawn Tennis Association tournament.

Now, as I close my journal, I see the MARTA bus turning onto the access road off U.S. 41. According to a printed schedule Annie D. has shown me on occasions too numerous to mention, Mr. Prober, the bus driver, is supposed to arrive at precisely 4:19 P.M. I watch Annie D. check her watch. She heaves her shoulders and makes another entry in her daily report to God on all that is not right with His world. "Six minutes late already!" she reports.

It is Annie D. who has shown the other maids and yardmen of Arcadia Heights exactly where Harold and I are basking in the afternoon sun. I see her shaking her head over what this world is coming to with spoiled rich women acting the way they do. That uppity Mrs. Bridges climbing a ladder to Mrs. Matthews's roof and dragging that lazy nigger Harold with her. "Thinking things through."

"And what," Annie D. surely asked Mrs. Matthews when Mrs. Matthews stopped by my house on the way to play tennis, "would a woman like Mr. Bridges's wife have to think things through about? That woman don't *need* to think! Her thinking time should have been whilst poor Mr. Bridges was still at home to do her thinking for her. You should have seen the way that poor man had to tell her everything she needed to know. What to cook for supper. Where to buy her clothes. How to raise those two children of his—'You shouldn't have never let Meg swing on that vine,' I told her—and why the wallpaper she tried to pick out for the dining room wasn't nothing a gentleman like Mr. Bridges would put up with in a dining room. 'Looks like *Chink* paper,' I told her. 'Chinese birds!' And that woman, she has a temper. She sure enough *does*."

I turn away from Annie D. and continue my story about what happened last night after Jimmy and I were escorted out of the club. About the way Jimmy dumped me on the sofa and left me to find the beginnings and the middles and the endings of all the dreams I dreamed after I realized he was keeping his bedroom door locked against me.

"It was only after I'd sorted out the one about swinging on the vine from the one about Mr. Bridges coming over to lecture me on vomiting," I tell Harold, "that I figured out what the answer taped to the ceiling of the isolation booth might have been."

When he doesn't answer, I grab the white butler's jacket I've been sitting on, drape it over Ida's weather vane, and crawl around to the other side of the chimney. Harold is lying on his back with his feet crossed at the ankles and his arms spread out like a crucified saint. His breathing is as loud as a snore.

I squat down beside him. "Listen, Harold. You need to hear this," I tell him, lifting his left eyelid. "The answer taped to the ceiling was a child's drawing."

Harold groans.

"It was the kind of child's drawing we used to do in Sunday School. Remember? With lots of squiggles and scrawls that may or may not have been an actual picture of God?"

Harold knocks my hand off his eyelid and mumbles something. It sounds like "Mudder."

5

"Stop being so paranoid," Ida said when I went over to see her yesterday morning. "Everybody in Atlanta isn't talking about what you did last night. You told me yourself that almost nobody even knows who you are anymore."

"Ha! So there you are, Margaret!" Arnold announced, coming out of the house to join his wife and me at the table on his patio. "I just hung up the phone from talking to Peter. Seems you made quite a scene at the club, honey. According to Bill Willowford, you emptied the dining room in sixty seconds flat."

I ignored Arnold's jovial chuckle and took a sip of coffee. "That man never liked me," I said after a moment. "And now Peter's going to kill me."

"I doubt it," Arnold said, still grinning. "Sounded to me like he thought it was pretty funny. Said it was exactly the sort of thing he'd have expected you to do."

I watched him tuck a napkin under his chin and begin digging into his pancakes. "What else did he say?" I asked, keeping my voice casual.

"Don't worry about it, sugar. We were just discussing business." Arnold looked over at Ida. "I'm trying to interest him in putting up some money for that new development, the one over in our old neighborhood." He reached for his glass of orange juice, took a swallow, and returned to his pancakes. "And to what do we owe the honor of your presence this morning, Margaret?" he asked, jabbing his fork in my direction. "You two girls have something cooked up for today?"

"I wanted to catch you before you left for work," I said. "You read contracts all the time, Arnold. I was hoping you'd read the separation agreement I signed yesterday and give me your professional opinion."

"I don't know," he said. "Leave me out of it. Peter's the one you should ask. He's the lawyer."

"Honestly!" Ida said, glaring at him. "That's the whole point. Margaret shouldn't be letting Peter set the terms. This is all his fault, not hers."

Arnold leaned back in his chair and patted his stomach. He'd put on quite a few pounds since the night I'd had a date with him on the beach at Sea Island.

"For God's sake," he said. "Get this sweet girl some breakfast, Ida, and then stay out of her business. It's none of our concern."

"Damn you, Arnold," she said, staying put in her chair. "If you don't want to read the agreement, then give Margaret the name of somebody good who will. Peter's not the only lawyer in the world. It shouldn't be hard to find one. Practically everyone we *know* is a lawyer."

But Arnold was already out of his chair and reaching for his briefcase. He gave Ida a quick kiss on the cheek. "By the way," he said, leaning over to pat me on the head, "I don't think there's such a thing as fault in divorce laws these days. You ought to talk to Peter about it, honey. He'd know."

I smiled my best Southern Belle smile and watched him waddle off toward the driveway.

I was thinking I might as well leave too when Little Arnold came outside. As he pulled out a chair and joined his mother and me at the table, I couldn't help thinking how handsome he'd become. He had his mother's dark hair and his father's pale complexion. He and Jimmy had been good friends all their lives. For

sixteen years I'd considered him practically one of my own chil-
dren. But lately things had changed. Since we'd moved in across
the street, Little Arnold had never once been inside our house.
I wondered how much he knew about Jimmy's father and me.
I reached across Big Arnold's empty plate and casually removed
Miss Grimsley's envelope before Little Arnold could see it.

"So how's it going, Mrs. Bridges?" he said.

"Fine, darling. Jimmy's fine, too. Why don't you two boys get
together today?"

"He has to clean out the pool," Ida said quickly.

I shot her a dirty look. I'd done everything I could to make
her encourage her son to include Jimmy in his plans, but Ida
preferred to pretend a mother couldn't tell a boy Little Arnold's
age who to run around with. The only hint she'd ever given me
was to suggest that perhaps Jimmy might fit in better with her
son's crowd of snobby, preppy Calvin Academy snots if he stopped
dressing like something out of *Soldier of Fortune* magazine.

"And when you're through with the pool," Ida said, ignoring
my look and turning to Little Arnold, "I need you to bring those
lawn chairs up from the basement for my garden club meeting
tomorrow."

"I'm leaving," I said. I didn't feel like spending one more
minute with Ida. I hated her for not seeing how much I needed
her son to be a friend to mine.

"But you can't leave yet!" she cried. She lowered her voice to a
whisper. "I haven't had a chance to read the *you know what.*"

"No," I said. "My head is splitting. And I promised Mary Earle
I'd drop by and see her this morning."

"Arnold?" Ida said, taking the separation agreement from my
lap. "Run upstairs and get Mrs. Bridges a couple of aspirins."

I snatched the envelope back and stood up. I should never have
confided in her. I resented the way she was always telling me what
to do. I loathed her husband for taking Peter's side against me.

"Please don't go," she said, following me to the driveway.
"Look, I'm sorry. Why don't you just stay for another cup of cof-

fee? We won't even think about that asshole Peter if you don't want to."

I didn't answer. I was halfway down the driveway before it occurred to me what I should have said to her. What I should have said was that if she wanted to talk about assholes she should talk about her own husband, not mine.

"The trouble with men like Arnold," I yelled back to her, "is you can't tell them anything! They know what they know, even if what they know is something they know absolutely nothing about!"

But Ida was no longer standing at the top of her driveway, and the only one who heard me was my next-door neighbor, poor old half-blind Mrs. Ferguson.

———

What Arnold Matthews didn't know one thing about was dreams. "You didn't mean to say 'concurrent,'" he'd told me one afternoon when I was in his backyard talking to Harold about the dream I kept having where I was swinging on a vine as big as a man's arm. "The word you meant to use, honey," Arnold informed me in that amused, condescending voice a good old boy always adopts when he needs to protect himself from becoming aware of his own ignorance, "is 'recurrent.'"

Since it was impossible to tell a man like Arnold something he didn't already know, I didn't bother to argue with him. But what I could have told him was that my dreams were often both recurrent *and* concurrent.

My dream about swinging on a vine in the woods across the street is often tangled up with the other recurrent dream I have, about Mary Earle Kennedy making mud pies on the bank of the creek. I've known Mary Earle and her twin sister, Joyce Belinda, for as long as I can remember. They grew up in the house down the street from me, next door to where Ida and her brother Shortie lived. Mary Earle was the little girl I was playing with one afternoon in the woods near the granite boulders—dropped out of nowhere in the middle of the pine grove—when my maid Beatrice suddenly grabbed our arms and whispered for us to squat down and *hush* and the next thing we knew we were watching in awe as two raccoons began mating on top of the boulders in a long, joyful *hmmmmm*. It was either then or a couple of years later that I confided to Mary Earle I was going to become a concert pianist when I grew up and Mary Earle confided to me she was going to be a singer holding a scarf in a dark café.

We were in the same Brownie troop. In grammar school we took ballet lessons together at Miss Dorothy's, and in junior high we learned the foxtrot and the jitterbug on the same dance floor above a liquor store in the heart of Buckhead. Mary Earle and I got married within a month of each other, and when our children were young we took turns baby-sitting. Over the years we were in the same provisional course with the Junior League, served on the same charity ball committees, spent a thousand hours together playing bridge and doing volunteer work at the Nearly New Shop.

We weren't best friends. We've always been too different for that. But *almost* best friends. For almost all our lives.

For the past few months I've been visiting Mary Earle every Thursday, rain or shine. On good days we sit at her kitchen counter making items for the annual Buckhead Garden Club bazaar. On bad days I sit beside her bed and drink iced tea while we rake up memories of when we were growing up and riding a Georgia Power bus downtown to the movies on Saturdays, sharing our Nancy Drew mysteries, giggling over the dirty jokes our older brothers taught us before we knew anything about inflammatory breast cancer or x-ray therapy or the kind of chemotherapy that can turn a roly-poly body like Mary Earle's into hard, stark lines, change a 1950s-style hairdo into a scarf wrapped around her head in a sad imitation of a gypsy fortune-teller.

As soon as I returned to my house from Ida's and woke up Jimmy, I drove over to my old neighborhood in Buckhead to visit Mary Earle. While I waited for Nurse Hatcher to greet me at the front door—"Oh, it's you"—I tried to think of something interesting to talk about. Except for occasional whispered remarks about the nurse, Mary Earle and I avoid unpleasant topics. She despises Nurse Hatcher, a huge stocky horse of a woman who keeps her patient entertained during the day by telling her about all the poor dead ladies she nursed before she came to nurse Mary Earle. She has a supply of stories about the husbands of these poor dears.

"*They* were the true sufferers, of course," she likes to explain, tossing her gray mane at the thought of all the husbands she's known personally who got to the point where they could hardly bring themselves to look at their dying wives. "You can't expect a man to be able to face that kind of upset the way a woman can," she says. "He's not built for it. And he has his work to do. It never surprises me one bit when a husband stops sleeping in the same room as his wife. It would be unnatural if he didn't."

"Don't listen to that bitch," I told Mary Earle as soon as I found her sitting at the kitchen counter. "She doesn't have the sense God gave a mule. Fire her. She's sadistic and stupid and she is very, very wrong, Mary Earle. Believe me. She's totally insane."

But Mary Earle has lost her will to fight against the mean insanities of Nurse Hatcher. In any case, she confided almost as soon as I sat down on a stool beside her, Nurse Hatcher was right. "Wallace doesn't sleep with me anymore," she whispered disconsolately. "He's afraid of me, Margaret. I scare him and the children to death."

Yes. I'd seen how Wally talked to Mary Earle now in a loud, booming voice that was as hollow as it was jolly. How Wally Junior and Courtney and Mary Joyce and Baby Sister tiptoed past their mother's room, pretending to their friends nothing was wrong; Mama was merely sleeping.

Mary Earle lowered her voice even further so Nurse Hatcher couldn't hear. "He never touches me down *there*," she whispered.

I never knew what to say when she confessed these intimate details of her marriage I didn't want to know. "Wally has always worshipped the ground you walk on," I told her. "He's always called you his pretty baby doll," I reminded her.

It was one of her better days. We began working on the tennis racket covers we'd decided to make out of gingham and felt for the next club bazaar.

"What should I do?" she asked after a few minutes.

It was the question she asked me most often. The one for which I never had an answer. I said nothing. Instead, I concentrated on sewing a white circle of felt on the racket cover without any of my stitches showing.

"And, Margaret . . ." she said.

"Yes?"

"I am outraged. I am simply out*raged*! Why did this happen to me? Can you answer me that? What have I ever done to deserve such a thing? Tell me! Haven't I always been a good wife and mother?"

"Yes."

"Haven't I always behaved like a lady?"

"Yes."

"And I'm a Christian. A devout *Catholic*!"

"Yes."

One "yes" too many.

"Don't patronize me," she said angrily, wadding the gingham in front of her into a ball. "I know you and Ida laugh at me behind my back. Don't you realize I've always known how you laugh at me? How you and Ida think I'm just a silly snob? Well, I can't help it. There are certain things in life worth being a snob *about*. But is that any reason why I should have to suffer? Oh! I find this entire thing *outrageous*."

I found it outrageous, too. And Mary Earle was right, of course. Ida and I had laughed at her behind her back ever since those days when we were little girls and Mary Earle insisted on wearing dotted swiss sundresses to play in the woods. And we laugh at her still. She begins wearing her full-length mink in October, no matter how warm the weather. She is still indignant over the hospital nurse who refused to allow her to wear her gold bracelets and her diamond rings into the operating room. "Our Buckhead pink," Ida and I call her. Still expecting others to come to her rescue. Still expecting others to do exactly as she commands.

Calling the fire department the time she couldn't figure out how to restart the pilot light on her furnace and she was afraid the house would explode. Phoning the police department the night Wally was out of town and her toy poodle ran away. And the fire department had come. The police department had come. Peter had come when Mary Earle wanted to sue the man who called her a fucking fool if she really believed she did not have to stop at four-way stop signs because gentlemen were supposed to yield to ladies.

Oh, my goodness, yes. Ida and I laugh about Mary Earle all the time. Our friendship with Mary Earle is based on a lifetime of needs and memories and habits that have become woven so tightly together that we rarely think any longer about all the un-pleasant subjects we dare not discuss: foreign people and new-rich people and people who use unengraved stationery. People who do not believe in the Immaculate Conception or the infallibility of a right-wing administration.

"And I keep telling Wallace to *do* something!" Mary Earle was saying in the kitchen. "And you know what Wallace does? He cries! That's what he does! I turn to my own husband, to the one person on earth who has taken a sacred vow before God and the Church to look after me until death do us part, and that is all he can think to do to save me. He cries!"

"Mary Earle," I said, helplessly. "Mary Earle."

"So you tell me what to do . . ." She unwadded the ball of ging-ham and began pressing it flat against the butcherblock counter with her fingers. "I know I'm supposed to be brave, Margaret. Father McCrory has instructed me it is my *duty* to be brave."

"No."

"And Dr. Fletcher has absolutely *forbidden* me to give up."

"Ah . . ."

"But I'm so frightened! And he says if I want to get well I have to keep a cheerful outlook, I have to convince my body to do its part and *try*."

"Yes."

"To fight back!"

"That's right."

"But how can I fight something that's everywhere? It's all over my body! How can I fight something I can't even see? Oh, dear Mother of God! I could kill this cancer! Margaret, I could take it in my bare hands and choke it to death. Whatever am I to do? You are my very best friend. You have an obligation to *tell* me."

Nurse Hatcher came charging into the room with her nostrils flaring. "No! No! No! No!" Her huge chest heaved with accusations. It was all my fault her patient had become so upset.

"I think we'd best be getting ourselves back to our bed," she said to Mary Earle, brushing past me and beginning to help Mary Earle down from her stool.

Mary Earle shot me a look of appeal. "Don't leave," she begged when Nurse Hatcher told me it was time for me to go. "Come back to my room in a minute. I need you to help me fix my face. Wallace is coming home for lunch. I want you to make me look pretty for him, Margaret."

"I keep telling Mary Earle she needs to get her beauty rest," Nurse Hatcher said as they left the room.

I stayed where I was. I listened to Nurse Hatcher clomping down the hallway toward the downstairs den that has been turned into Mary Earle's bedroom. While I waited to give her enough time to settle Mary Earle in her satin bed jacket against her silk pillowcase, I studied the kitchen. My old friend's choice of weapons was exactly the kind of silly, scatterbrained weapon a middle-aged Buckhead pink would think to use.

"When are you going to grow up, Mary Earle?" I asked her furiously when I entered the den. "You couldn't kill anything with your bare hands if your life depended on it."

Mary Earle raised her head from her pillow.

"How can you expect to fight something you haven't even bothered to visualize?" I asked her while I put on her makeup. "You have to concentrate, Mary Earle. You can't expect other people to do *everything* for you. If you want to use a weapon, use something that makes sense. Use your *brain*. See the cancer in your mind's eye as something you hate so much you're going to get rid of it if it's the last thing you do. And then get rid of it! Put it in your trashmasher. Or down the garbage disposal. Or burn it from the inside out in your microwave oven. There are probably a hundred ways you could visualize murdering it that are better than trying to murder it with your bare hands. What is the matter with you?"

Mary Earle did not answer.

Oh, Mary Earle.

I lay down beside her on the bed. I was overwhelmed with sadness, with the hopelessness of trying to cure anything with ideas from how-to books.

"I'm sorry," I said. I took her hand. When Meg died, Mary Earle had embarrassed me with her awkward attempts to console me. Her platitudes had made me cringe. But she had been there. She had let me know how much she cared. "Forgive me, Mary Earle," I said. "I'm truly sorry. I was being stupid. Crazy. I don't know what you should . . ."

"Shhhhh!" She closed her eyes. After a few minutes she said: "Yes." Her voice was imperious. "My new Deluxe Cuisinart. I see it quite clearly now."

I waited for what seemed a long time.

Suddenly Mary Earle grabbed my arm. "Oh, Margaret!" she cried out, laughing. "I love it! Puree of Nurse Hatcher! Don't you love it?"

Yes. I loved it. And we were laughing. We were hugging ourselves with laughter. We hardly noticed poor Wally tiptoeing to the foot of the bed, hangdogged with fright and despair.

"Old horse's ass Hatcher!" I cried. "Now she can go and be with all those poor dears she keeps talking about. It's where she belongs."

"Isn't that the truth?" Mary Earle shot back.

I looked to the foot of the bed in time to catch Wally's expression turning from puzzlement to hope.

"I swear to goodness, Margaret!" Mary Earle squealed triumphantly. "Isn't that just the absolute gospel *truth*?"

6

As I backed my station wagon out of the Kennedys' driveway and headed down the street to visit my parents, I realized that for the first time since Peter moved out I felt hopeful. "Visualize success," the author of Ida's book had advised. Only my own stubbornness had kept me from seeing that this was really no different from what my father had tried to teach me all my life. "Courage, frankness, and good cheer, Margaret! We are the gods of the chrysalis."

When I walked up to the front door of my childhood home, I made a point of lengthening my stride, of swinging my arms confidently. I pictured myself as a carefree divorcee, one of those women with long painted fingernails and enormous cleavage and the kind of sparkling personality that scares her married friends to death.

As usual, I found Daddy sitting in his red leather chair in the den, staring at the television set. He may or may not have understood what I said when I bent down to kiss him on the cheek. "So, how are you doing today?" I said. "It's Margaret."

"Your daddy's doing good today," his nurse answered, closing her crossword puzzle book. She glanced over at Daddy. "Tell your daughter how good you're doing, Mr. Hunter."

"Well, fine!" I said, completing the litany Betty and I had established over the past year. "That's real fine."

I sat with them until we'd seen the prize behind curtain number three, and then I walked down the back hallway looking for Mother. I'd thought of some more lies I could tell her to reassure her about my separation agreement. I found her in the breakfast room, sitting at the table. She didn't ask about the agreement, however. She wanted to know what I'd worn to the club the night before.

"My blue cocktail dress, I think."

"And Jimmy?"

"The gray suit you bought him for his birthday."

"Lovely." She walked over to the shelves under the breakfast room window and began searching through her cookbooks. "By the way," she said, running her finger down the index page of *1001 Ways to Please a Husband*, "your father and I have been worried about him, Margaret."

"Who? Jimmy?"

"Yes." She reached for another book without looking at me. "Is he mad at us about something? He hasn't been by to visit his grandfather in over a month."

I couldn't very well tell her that since her grandchild's recent decision to adopt a cheerful "everything's going to be all right" attitude, he no longer believed in being reminded of anything unpleasant. Instead, I provided other excuses on my child's behalf: exams, spring break, his work in the basement darkroom. "You know how children are these days," I said.

"Ah, well. It's not important."

She put aside the cookbooks and went into the kitchen. When she returned with our cups of coffee, she said, "There was something else I wanted to ask you, dear."

"Yes, Mother?"

But apparently it had skipped her mind. Instead of asking me a question, she began reminiscing about when I was a child and how terrible it had been for everyone because there seemed to be so many more diseases going around then. "The polio epidemic was dreadful. We were almost afraid to let you and Buford out of the house. And, of course, there was rubella—I have no idea if children still get that or not—and the other type of measles that you and Buford caught when you were both quite small, while I was still off recuperating from tuberculosis. And chicken pox, naturally. And the mumps. And that nasty skin disease children used to get where they had to go to the school nurse and be painted with gentian violet."

"Ringworm," I said.

"Yes . . ." she agreed in a distracted voice. She sighed and looked over at my empty cup. "More coffee, darling?"

"No, I guess I better go. I'm supposed to be meeting somebody for lunch at Clarence Foster's."

"Good, dear. I've always loved that restaurant." She rose somewhat reluctantly from her chair and followed me down the hallway. At the front door she stopped me by putting her hand on my arm. "Not that it's important, Margaret, but I just remembered what I meant to ask you on the phone last night."

I took a deep breath. "Yes?"

"Your father and I have been trying to come up with the name of Mary Earle's twin sister."

I laughed with relief. "Honestly, Mother! You've known Joyce Belinda all her life. That's who I'm having lunch with."

"No. Her last name."

"Johnson. She's married to Jason Johnson, Peter's golfing buddy. Remember? The one I told you about whose clothing business went bankrupt last year? Actually, I'm not all that happy with Joyce Belinda. She hasn't spoken to Mary Earle for over a month, not since Jason asked Wally for a job and didn't get one. That's why I'm taking Joyce Belinda to lunch. I want to tell her to stop being such a snot. 'For crying out loud,' I'm going to tell her. 'Mary Earle is dying. Can't you get that through your stupid head?' "

"I don't know," Mother said. "Maybe you ought to keep out of it, dear." She began twisting her wedding band around and around on her finger. "I hate to say it, Margaret, but you've always had this propensity to go around saving people, you've been like that since you were a child. I used to tell your father we could depend on Buford to bring home stray animals and Margaret to bring home stray people. I'll never forget that time you brought over some poor girl to play with you who had ringworm all over her head."

"That was Joyce Belinda, Mother."

"Yes. Well, I was just thinking about her because I forgot to tell you I ran into her yesterday while I was playing bridge at the club and she happened to mention that she and her husband had been invited to have drinks the other night in those new condominiums down the street from the Peachtree Battle Shopping Center. You know the ones I mean? Where they tore down the old Collier mansion?"

I opened the front door and stepped out onto the veranda. "Listen, Mother. I wish I could hear about it, but I'm already late."

She followed me out to the car, still talking.

"And the girl who owned the condominium, Joyce Belinda said, had done everything up in blue. Blue walls, blue carpet, blue upholstery . . ."

I turned on the ignition and waited for Mother to take her hand off the window.

"You know, Margaret, I've never really liked Mary Earle's twin sister all that much. She's rather a gossip, don't you think? And she was never your best friend. Remember?"

Yes. I remembered. She'd always had a mean streak. Unlike Mary Earle, Joyce Belinda had always been the kind of fluffy-headed Buckhead pink who was too dangerous to laugh at behind her back.

"Ah, well," Mother said. "Never mind. I'm sure everything is going to work out all right." She patted the side of my car and then stepped back on the sidewalk.

I decided not to hear whatever else Joyce Belinda had said that my mother had forgotten to tell me over the telephone. I stomped on the gas pedal and sped away.

———————

She was waiting for me at a table toward the back of the restaurant and making every effort to prove that not all twins are identical. Mary Earle would have been wearing one of those outfits Ida called "Mary Earle's frills and foo-foo." Probably something pink. Joyce Belinda, on the other hand, was a vision of gray: gray suit, gray blouse, and short, curly hair as gray as nature had intended.

"You look great," I said, sliding into the booth.

"And you look awful," she answered. She shook her head in disbelief. "You must have lost twenty pounds since I last saw you."

I shrugged and glanced at the man sitting alone at a table near our booth. He reminded me of Peter; he was wearing a white band of skin around his finger where a wedding band had recently been.

"So, is the divorce final?" Joyce Belinda asked as soon as the waiter had left with our orders. "Jason and I keep thinking we ought to have you over or something. Poor Margaret! I had no idea you'd be so *thin*."

"There's not going to be a divorce necessarily," I said. "We're just having a trial separation."

"And I feel so sorry for Jimmy. He used to be such a *sweet* child before his father deserted him. But someone told me they saw him at the club last night and he looked almost *belligerent*."

"It's just his clothes, Joyce Belinda. You know boys. They go through all kinds of stages." I lowered my voice so she would lower hers. "And nobody's deserted anybody. He sees Peter all the time."

"Well, you ought to do something about that boy. I can assure you I'd never let a child of *mine* shave his head. If a child of mine even *thought* about shaving his head, he'd soon have another thought coming."

I made no comment. The only child Joyce Belinda and Jason Johnson had was Lucie Earle, a pretty girl with her aunt's baby-doll complexion and her father's sharp wit. She'd been Meg's best friend; they'd planned to room together at college.

"I'm afraid when it comes to teaching a child how to dress and how to behave like a gentleman," Joyce Belinda was saying, "you know as well as I do that it's always up to the mother."

Again, I made no comment. And after the waiter brought our salads, I remained mostly silent and listened to Joyce Belinda talk nonstop at the top of her lungs—the man at the next table kept leaning forward to catch every word—until our plates were removed and our entrees were presented.

I didn't really blame her for changing the subject every time I now tried to bring up her sister's name, but I began to wonder at the subjects she changed to. ("I *adore* Lucie Earle's roommate. She's from *Montana*, of all places . . ." "Have you seen your old house? Don't you just *love* the way they've torn down that ugly back porch stoop you used to have and put up a deck across the back?")

As I watched Joyce Belinda stab her fork into a bite of sauteed crab and bring it to her mouth in the European fashion she and Mary Earle had adopted ever since their junior year abroad, I thought about how my mother always turned out to be right. No, Joyce Belinda had never been a best friend. And she was a terrible gossip.

"By the way," she was saying, "I guess you've heard about Bobby Turner."

I shook my head.

"He's given his Phi Delt pin to a darling little girl from Talla-hassee."

Yes. And Joyce Belinda was mean.

"Listen," I said, trying one last time to change the conversation, "I want to talk about Mary Earle. I saw her this morning and she was looking somewhat better, I thought. She was wearing the satin bed jacket Wally gave her last month for her birthday.

You know? The one with the embroidered roses? She looked so pretty."

"Pretty?" Joyce Belinda put down her fork and glared at me. "Mary Earle is an absolute *skeleton*. I *warned* her about drinking all that coffee, everybody *knows* it causes breast cancer, but she went right ahead and drank it anyway."

"I'm sure it must be terribly sad for you to see your sister like this, terribly frightening, but—"

"You don't know the first thing about it."

"I know she's unhappy. I know there are things she wants to tell you that she can't tell anyone else. And she's worried about what's going to happen to the children, Joyce Belinda. I think she wants to ask you to look after Wally."

"Wally? I couldn't look after that man if he were the last person on earth. When Jason lost his business, Wally was secretly *glad*."

"Now, you know that's not true. He—"

"Don't bother to take up for him, Margaret. He's been jealous of Jason ever since we got married. Oh! I want you to know I literally crawled on my hands and knees to my sister—she's always had Wally wrapped around her finger, she could have *made* him give Jason a job!—but this was their chance to rub their victory in. I'll never forgive them for that. Wally's been against us both from the start. They had two children before he finally allowed Mary Earle to name one after me. And that was *years* after Lucie Earle was born. Oh, Wally Kennedy has never shown me the *least* kindness."

"Come on," I said. "That doesn't have anything to do with what's happening now. Mary Earle's dying, damn it! Can't you understand that simple fact? Make up with her before it's too late, for God's sake." I reached across the table and gripped her arm. "She's only got a few more weeks. A couple of months at best."

Joyce Belinda flushed and jerked her arm away. "Instead of sitting here lecturing *me*," she said angrily, grabbing the check from the waiter and shoving it across the table to me, "you ought to be doing something about *yourself*." She was trembling with rage. "As I told your mother yesterday, if you knew what was good for you, you'd be out hiring a private detective."

"What?"

She pushed her chair back and stood up. "I can assure you I'd never let a husband of *mine* run around on me behind my back."

The man at the next table grinned.

"If a husband of mine even *dreamed* of having an affair with some young twenty-six-year-old career woman, he'd wish he were *dead*."

I felt my face redden. My knees began to shake. I watched myself figuring the tip. Twenty times thirty was six dollars, divided by two was . . .

"Did you know Peter invited Jason and me over to her condominium for drinks the other night? It was . . ."

I didn't listen. If I listened, everything that was happening might turn out to be true. I watched myself following Joyce Belinda out of the restaurant, watched myself wandering through the parking lot, trying to find my car.

"Her name is Sydney Roberts," Joyce Belinda shouted in my ear. "And let me tell you, she's *most* attractive . . ."

I unlocked my car door and slid behind the steering wheel. I put the key in the ignition.

She leaned her head through the open window. "By the way, Margaret," she said, her voice steely with outrage. "I don't need you to tell *me* about breast cancer, thank you very much! It's contagious in my family. I'll have you know I had to watch my mother *die* of breast cancer."

I backed the car out of the parking space with her hand still on the window.

"The next time you decide to tell me how to behave toward my own *sister*, you can kindly step straight to *hell*."

I slammed on the accelerator, roared around the rows of parked cars.

"What makes you think *you* have a right to tell anybody else what to do?" I heard a voice screaming after me. "Why, you didn't even know enough to look after your own *daughter*!"

Sometimes when I am in my fog, I sit very still for a long, long time and do nothing at all. Other times, I do anything that comes to mind. As I turned onto Peachtree Street with the screams of Joyce Belinda pounding in my head, what came to mind was some advice Daddy used to always give me: "Remember, happiness doesn't depend on who you are or what you have, Margaret. It depends solely upon what you think."

Yes. Mr. Carnegie and Daddy were right. Let's not be bitter, I decided to think. There are no villains here, no heroines. Life is full of change, I should have explained to Joyce Belinda, "and this latest change may well turn out to be one of those opportunities of a lifetime I keep reading about in *Ms.* magazine. I might go back to college. Or I might pursue music again—I once played the piano rather nicely."

No. I was not nearly so tragic a figure as the first Margaret, who gave birth to seven children and saw five of them die in infancy. And I was certainly no more pathetic than any other girl our age who had once believed she was merely doing the proper thing when she married too young and dropped out of Sweet Briar to put her husband through law school. I was no more irrelevant, I should have assured Joyce Belinda, than any other girl our age who did not have the luxury of growing up in a different time altogether than a certain Dr. Sydney Roberts. Why, when I was in my twenties it had never once occurred to me that I should have been preparing myself to become an important career personage. That instead of raising children and working at the Nearly New Shop, I could have been pursuing personal fulfillment by saving lives during the day and at night enjoying sex out of wedlock with a Nothing-but-a-Homemaker's husband!

Yes. Sometimes when I am in a fog, I do nothing at all. This time I found a phone booth and called Ida.

"She knows," I said, struggling to hear my voice. "Joyce Belinda's been telling everybody in Atlanta about Peter and Sydney. She's even told my mother."

"Snap out of it!" Ida ordered curtly. "Where are you calling from?"

I glanced around. Somewhere in Buckhead. What difference did it make? I was at a Shell station. Maybe Gulf.

"What did you say, Margaret?"

"No. It's the Chevron station next to the Peachtree Battle Shopping Center. Oh, my God," I moaned. "Mothers always learn the truth whether they want to or not."

"Wait there for me. I'm coming to get you. Okay? I know just what to do."

But there was nothing to do, I was going to tell Ida as soon as she arrived. The only thing to do was to drive downtown to the new Atlanta library and jump from the roof the way my Grandmother Leticia had jumped from the roof of the old Atlanta library before me.

"Good grief," Ida said thirty minutes later when she found me still standing in the phone booth. "Get in this car and wipe that pitiful expression off your face. Trust me. This is going to be fantastic, like old times. Remember? All those Nancy Drew mysteries we used to read? Now, I'll be Nancy," she said, screeching onto Peachtree Street, "and you can be her best pal George."

"I don't want to be George," I said sullenly. "When Meg used to read Nancy Drews, she always suspected that George was a lesbian."

Ida was leaning forward, her head barely able to peer above the steering wheel of her Jaguar. "Oh, this is perfect! Sydney works all day. She won't find out in a million years."

"This isn't one of your best ideas, Ida," I murmured. "If Peter learns about it . . ."

Ida slammed on her brakes at a red light. "I don't know what's happened to you. You used to be fun, downright *insane*. But now you're acting like a spoiled brat. If you can't be a good sport, I'll just drive you back to your car."

But I could tell Ida was not about to turn around. She was racing down Peachtree again, weaving in and out of traffic like a maniac. "Now, just keep your mouth shut for once," she warned me as she suddenly cut the wheel and roared into a driveway marked *Private*. "Let me handle this."

The guard at the gate was young. Blond. Male. The kind of young blond male who has no problem understanding interior decorators who arrive at their clients' condominiums without a way to get in.

"Happens all the time," he said, handing Ida the passkey. "I always say you have to make allowances for artistic temperaments."

I wasn't so sure.

"Wait," I whispered when I realized we'd already parked the car and that the hallway Ida was leading me down probably ended with Sydney's door. "What if she comes home unexpectedly and catches us? We need to agree on what we're going to say to her if that happens. Some alibi that will stand up in court. You know?"

Ida didn't answer. She was too busy staring at Sydney's living room.

For a moment I forgot Meg had died and I actually saw myself hurrying home to tell her about it. "Oh, you should have been there, Meg! It was like standing on the bottom of the deep end of the club swimming pool. Remember? Everything was slick and shiny. Everything that wasn't slick and shiny was *blue*."

The furniture seemed to be floating in water. I floated with it, drowning in blue carpet, blue walls, blue upholstery . . .

"Well. Don't just stand there gasping for air," Ida said. "Find the medicine cabinet. That's what you're always snooping through when you go to other people's houses." She had crossed to the opposite side of the room and was already rummaging through the drawers of a desk. "Oh! I told you this was going to be fantastic!" she said over her shoulder. "She's got letters from her mama."

I didn't move. I was staring at a pile of record albums on a blue plexiglass table.

"Or go look in her refrigerator. See what she eats."

She ate black lettuce. A quarter-pound of margarine. Umpteen cans of Peter's favorite beer. In the sink I found the remains of the night they'd entertained Joyce Belinda and Jason: four highball glasses and a plate with a dab of something white on it that tasted like it had been either Camembert or Brie. I rinsed off the dishes and lay them down on a towel to dry.

"Listen to this!" I heard Ida calling. "She's told her mother that Peter is thirty-six!"

I wandered into the next room and began making up her bed. The sheets looked familiar. White with blue monograms: MHB. There were no books on the bedside table. The reading lamp had a motel light bulb in it: 25-watt.

"Oh, this is wonderful, Margaret!" Ida called. "Sydney thinks Peter is a prominent trial attorney who defends poor people!"

Sydney had dropped the clothes she'd worn the day before in the middle of the floor. I picked them up: padded bra, size 32A; control-top pantyhose, underpanties that smelled reasonably clean. No slip. Her white cotton uniform had stains under the armpits.

"Come in here quick!" Ida cried. "You've got to see this! She thinks her checking account balance is one hundred and eighty-seven dollars, but she doesn't know how to subtract!"

I wondered where Sydney kept her washing machine.

"And she owes everybody in town. There's a Rich's bill that's been due since February!"

Peter's old loafers were thrown under a chair next to the closet. He did not keep his suits in Sydney's apartment apparently. The only hanger belonging to him held one of his running outfits. In the chest of drawers, he'd folded a pair of jockey shorts next to a rumpled nightgown.

"Margaret? Are you listening? What are you doing in there?"

What I was doing was folding Sydney's nightgown and re-arranging her dresser drawers. And then what I was doing was staring at her medical diploma hanging on the wall above the dresser: Sydney Millicent Roberts, X-ray Technician.

"I guess Peter never actually told me she was a doctor," I confessed to Ida on the way back to pick up my car at the service station. "I guess when he said she did something medical, I just assumed the worst."

"I love it!" Ida cried. "He must have met her that time he thought he had an ulcer."

"Two months ago," I said, closing my eyes so I could try to visualize their first date together. I supposed Peter would be lying on his side on a table with his right knee drawn up to his chest. He'd look worried. *There now*, I murmured to him, playing the role of Sydney. I smiled and lifted the sheet covering his but-tocks. *Time to take your medicine like a brave little boy*, I crooned encouragingly as I started the barium enema . . .

"You'd think a man as intelligent as Peter would have sense enough to stay away from a girl whose people don't know enough to teach her to put on a slip when she's wearing a white uni-form," Ida said. "And don't you just adore the way all her record albums are either Barbra Streisand or your entire collection of what's-his-name?"

"Ashkenazy." I reached over and turned on the car radio. " 'Slip slidin' away,' " I sang along merrily. "That whole tacky plexiglass living room was just slip slidin' away, Ida!"

We laughed.

"She keeps a set of extra fingernails in her medicine cabinet," I said. "And she's being treated for a vaginal yeast infection."

"And have you ever in your life seen anything to beat those letters her mama wrote her? That poor woman! She thinks you're *dead*."

"Ah, well. Maybe it's best for poor Peter that I passed away."

"Oh, my goodness, yes! Her mama has met dozens of ladies like you through the movies." Ida mimicked the Yankee voice we'd heard in the letters: "'His wife sounds like she must have been one of those dreadful southern creatures boys marry when they're too young to know any better . . .'"

We reached the gas station, still laughing. I got out of Ida's car and opened the door to my station wagon.

"Wait!" Ida called. She leaned out the window. "In case you didn't know it, your kind of creature is notoriously shallow and empty-headed!"

I tooted the horn and drove off to the music of Meg's favorite singer. One of the easy-listening radio stations was devoting an hour to Paul Simon's greatest hits. *Step out the back, Jack. Make a new plan, Stan. There must be fifty ways to leave your lover . . .*

Yes. "Fifty ways at least," I said out loud.

More ways than Meg's father had ever bothered to imagine.

1. Strangulation
2. Suffocation
3. Asphyxiation
4. Starvation

As I drove down Northside Drive on my way to U.S. 41, I refused to think about what else Sydney's mother had mentioned in her letters. "You must be particularly sensitive to this man's needs," she'd written. "Everybody knows how much these southern women like to tease, but as poor Peter probably discovered all too soon in his marriage, they almost always turn out to be F-R-I-G-I-D."

5. Conflagration
6. Amputation
7. Radiation

I concentrated on my driving. "Dehydration . . ."

Yes. And at the point of death, Sydney's life would flash before her. All the fragments of her memories would lead her to the overwhelming questions: Why? What if? Honestly, what?

And she might find the answers worth dying for. She could watch the obligatory scenes of her life reveal themselves in proper sequence. She would see it all. So this is what happened! Why did I refuse so long to believe it? The ending was predestined from the beginning, after all.

At her young age, she would have fewer scenes to examine than I would, of course. And could I know, even as I was dying, that the scenes were true and not just somebody else's version of my past? A version told me by others through family stories, through photographs of a child sitting in her grandmother's high chair and banging a spoon against a silver dish? A little girl with red hair hanging in her face—her sundress slipping off one shoulder—daring the eye behind the camera to make a permanent record of this moment in which she is standing, hands on hips, beside a uniformed black maid in front of some forgotten oak tree in some forgotten neighborhood park?

And even if I could recall that moment, or the moment years later when I stood with a gloved hand on the arm of the stranger I'd gone and married, or lay in a hospital bed holding the daughter we had conceived, would I be sure I was remembering these moments without the biases of all I'd learned, and unlearned, since?

THINGS I MEANT TO DO

1. *Ask Meg and Jimmy if they ever found a cigar box full of minié balls and arrowheads I hid in the Indian cave near the creek when I was a little girl.*
2. *Locate the missing talking doll.*
3. *Get Peter to explain to me why he never told me before we married that twenty-three years later he was going to become an unfaithful, cowardly, immature, controlling, neurotic, compulsive, unethical, condescending, pompous, insensitive, selfish, impatient, chauvinistic, oversexed prig.*

They almost always turn out to be F-R-I-G-I-D.

I went over the list again. Things I meant to do before it was too late.

   4. Lie naked on the beach. Let the incoming tide wash over my body . . .

7

"Remember?" I'd meant to ask Ida after I'd been downtown to sign the separation agreement with Peter. "Remember when we were all in the ninth grade and we went to the old Loew's Grand Theater and fell in love with that scene in *From Here to Eternity*? The one where Deborah Kerr and Burt Lancaster were lying half-naked on the beach while the tide washed over their bodies?

But as I drove down U.S. 41 on my way back to Arcadia Heights, I remembered why I hadn't asked. That scene no longer seemed as erotic to me as it had when I was fourteen. No. That scene now struck me as being rather sad. It made me feel guilty.

Because after you've been married a long time, you realize making love doesn't always happen when and how you used to dream it would happen when you were young and virginal. After you've been married for twenty-two or twenty-three years, a scene like that just makes you start thinking about salt water getting into Deborah's nose, or fiddler crabs crawling around in her hair, or wet sand working its way up inside her crotch.

No. Making love was not always the way you'd dreamed it would be even when you were doing it in a comfortable bed with dry sheets. Sometimes when you are making love you get chronic cystitis, like Ida. Or your back gets out of whack, like Arnold. Or you're sick all over your body, like Mary Earle. Or frightened all over your body, like Wally.

Or sometimes you're in grief. And when you are grieving, one of you may not feel the same way at the same time as the other one of you who is grieving. One of you may just want to lie quietly on her back under the father of her first-born child who died and do nothing at all. And the other one of you may want to do everything in a hurry. He may need to get back at his daughter's death by proving to himself, with angry, pain-inflicting thrusts, that he, at least, is still alive.

And after you've made love, the one who is in a rage may roll over on his side, without a word to comfort you, and start sobbing. And the one who is still on her back may be empty of all thought and feeling except for the insistent ache that begins as one finger pressing down on her chest and then gradually expands into a fist that seems to take forever to knead her into dreams about *whys* and *if onlys*.

Yes. After you've been married a long time, the thought of making love can cause you to become anxious. After you've been married for twenty-three years, the idea of having to make love again can cause you to feel depressed. Tired. Extremely hostile.

———

"I don't understand what you're so furious about," Meg had said the morning she died. "I'm only doing what you always taught me I should do."

"No, darling," I said. "You've got it all wrong. I never meant *you*, Meg. I was talking about other kinds of girls."

She didn't answer. She was furious, too. Embarrassed.

I sat on her bed and watched her pulling her nightshirt over her head, fastening her bra, slipping her thin legs into faded jeans.

"Why must you always take everything I tell you so literally, Meg? The only reason I ever told you about sex when you were growing up was to keep you from doing it until you were grown. You're only a child. You have plenty of time for this when you're older."

She grabbed a T-shirt from a pile of clothes on the chair in front of her dressing table.

"I don't know what to say to you anymore, Meg. Tell me what

I can say to make you change your mind before it's too late."

She went into the bathroom.

"Are you going to talk to me about this?" I called to her through the open door. "If your father knew you'd been to see Dr. Davison, he'd kill you and me both."

I heard her brushing her teeth. Gargling. Where had I gone wrong? What had I told her all those years ago when she came home with that crazy story she'd learned from some child in the fourth grade? "It's not nasty, Meg, it's beautiful," I'd probably told her. "It's something two people do when they're in love." What had I said when she was twelve and begged for a sister? "You don't make a baby every time. You have to be ovulating, remember?" Oh, my God.

"It wasn't Peggy's fault," I'd told Meg when a girl in her junior class at Calvin Academy got pregnant. "If her mother wasn't such a prude, she would have had enough sense to teach her daughter about birth control."

Meg was back in the room, kneeling in front of me and retrieving her tennis shoes from under the bed.

"Did Dr. Davison explain about the possible side effects?" I asked.

Silence.

"Listen, Meg. They don't know *beans* about the side effects! Twenty years from now you could get cancer from those pills. Do you realize that? Twenty years from now you could be dying like Mrs. Kennedy. And for what? You and Bobby will probably never see each other again after you go off to college."

Meg grabbed a hairbrush from the dressing table. Her neck was flushed.

"Come on, darling," I said. "You're too smart to be dumb."

She bent at the waist, flipped her long red hair over the back of her head, and began brushing. I counted the strokes under my breath to keep from screaming at her.

Nine . . . ten . . . eleven . . .

"If you didn't want me to know, Meg, you should have kept your book closed. Damn it! I wish you hadn't left it in the Secret

Room wide open for me to read. What a thing for a mother to find written in the margin of *Pride and Prejudice*! Do you think I'm an idiot? Do you honestly believe I'm too dense to figure out "Dr. Davison. Monday. Two o'clock"?

She walked out of the room without speaking.

"He brought you into this world!" I screamed after her. I picked up the hairbrush and threw it down the stairs after her. "I'm going to strangle that man for giving my teenaged daughter birth control pills!"

She started running.

"Do you hear me, Meg?" I ran after her. "I forbid it!"

She snatched her jacket from the table in the breakfast nook. Yes. She was furious. Embarrassed. Maybe a little frightened at herself.

"Wait," I said. "Do you want Bobby to think you're that kind of girl?"

"Ha!" Jimmy laughed. He was leaning against the kitchen sink, smirking.

Meg stopped at the back door, swung around, and faced me.

"Right, Mom," she said. "I'm that kind of girl. I'm the kind of girl you raised me to be. Remember? The kind who doesn't sit around expecting other people to make up her mind for her? So I'm only doing what you taught me to do. Okay? I'm being responsible for my own actions, I'm not leaving everything up to some boy."

"But that's *years* away, Meg."

"I love Bobby now, and he loves me."

"What on earth can you know about love at your age? You hardly know him."

"In case you haven't noticed," she said, jerking open the door, "girls have changed. You talk a good story, but under all that mother-daughter advice of yours you're still the same old Buckhead pink you were when you first met Daddy."

"You're darned right I'm a pink! I waited until I was almost married!"

She slammed the door behind her.

"Where does she think she's going?" I said to Jimmy. I shoved him away from the sink and looked out the window. Meg was running across the street, scrambling down the embankment into the woods.

"You go get your sister and tell her I said to come back here this instant!"

"Aw, Mom."

"And don't argue. I will not have her running out on me when I still have plenty more to say."

I'm sorry, I said all those hours later when we found Jimmy kneeling in shock beside her body. *It was all my fault, darling.*

"There, Walter," Mother said, taking my grief-stricken father by the arm. "There, there, darling."

I listened to the crows cawing from the pine trees, the snap of branches under our feet, the rustle of the underbrush as we made our way through the woods up to the street. Our neighbors were waiting for us. They stood in quiet circles, avoiding our eyes.

"Just for the record," a policeman said to Jimmy, "why were you two kids in the woods?"

Jimmy doubled over at the waist and hugged himself. "It was just this place," he mumbled. "It was just this place where we used to play when we were children."

The policeman put his hand on Jimmy's shoulder. "Go on, son."

"So we were just sitting around talking for a while. In the pine grove. And then we went down to the train trestle to see if the hobo fires were still there. And then . . ."

"No!" I cried, hearing my son's voice falter. "It was all my fault! Leave him alone!"

Jimmy shook his head miserably. "And so then . . . we found the old path that leads over to the creek . . . and the big oak tree was still there . . ." His voice broke. He looked up and appealed to me with his eyes. "Remember, Mom?"

Yes. When he and Meg were young, I'd shown them how their Uncle Buford used to take a Boy Scout hatchet and chop the bottoms off the huge vines that hung from the upper branches. I'd shown them how, if they stood on a certain limb near the top of the tree, they could swing all the way down across the creek bed.

"Christ," Peter groaned beside me.

I turned to see what he was looking at. Behind us, the men were bringing Meg's body out of the woods in a green plastic bag. I reached out to Jimmy. "Don't look," I warned him.

But he was already staring at the stretcher, and when I tried to fold him in my arms he jerked away and began running toward the house. Peter ran after him.

I stood where I was. I needed to make sure the men steadied her body as they loaded it into the back of the ambulance.

"What was the victim's full name, Mrs. Bridges?" I heard someone asking.

I didn't answer. I needed to watch the ambulance pull away from the curb and begin making it's way up the winding oak-canopied street. I needed to make sure the driver wasn't going to suddenly start speeding.

"What was her address?"

"It was an accident," I said quietly, looking at the policeman. "The rest doesn't matter."

"Don't!" I cried to Peter in bed that night after he'd talked to Jimmy and learned the details. "I don't want to hear. She's dead. Isn't that all a mother needs to know?"

I rolled over on my side and waited for the ache in my chest to expand into a fist. Behind me, Peter was sobbing.

———

I was in such a fog as I followed Ida's car down U.S. 41, I forgot to watch her and drove a mile past the access road exit. I didn't realize my mistake until I found myself crossing the bridge over the Chattahoochee River. By the time I could stop crying long enough to see a place to turn around, it was after four o'clock. It was almost four-fifteen when I finally reached the gates of Arcadia Heights. As I turned into my driveway, the MARTA bus was just pulling away from the curb across the street. Harold waved to me out the window. I may or may not have waved back.

Little Arnold was in old Mrs. Ferguson's front yard next door playing catch football with Mrs. Ferguson's grandchild Billy. "Damn you!" I wanted to scream at them. "Play with *Jimmy!*"

The Spitfire was parked in the garage. I practiced what I was going to say to my son before his father arrived to take him away to Lake Burton for the weekend.

"Listen, Jimmy. I've changed my mind," I was going to say. "I want to know everything that occurred that day in the woods. I want to know how Meg happened to fall from the vine, and how she looked when she fell, and whether she said anything to you before she died." And then I was going to say, "I'm sorry. For everything I've ever done wrong, son, I'm just extremely sorry."

But when I entered the house, I discovered he'd gone. He'd left a message for me under Annie D.'s Smiley Face magnet. "Left early with Dad. Back on Sunday."

I fixed myself a drink and wandered from the kitchen into the dining room. I had the house to myself. Nobody around to tell me what to do. A good three hours of freedom before I had to decide whether or not I wanted to go to the party my brother and his wife were having for the famous spiritualist who had moved into their neighborhood.

What does a man want? I asked myself as I stared at the wallpaper Peter had picked out for the dining room. The faces of the men on horseback, chasing their hounds around the room, gave no clues. The fox was apparently in hiding.

I stopped in front of the mantel in the living room to look up at the portrait of the baby Margaret I was named after. She sat on Katherine's lap, dressed like a miniature adult. "Poor child," I murmured. "Doomed to spend eternity holding a pomegranate you will never taste."

I walked across the room to the doorway of Peter's study to see what Katherine looked at all day: books on the recessed shelves, fake logs in the fireplace, Windsor chairs, a carpet that absorbed my footsteps like a sponge. My grand piano in the corner. "Poor thing," I said. "Poor old neglected thing."

I sat down on the bench and listened as my fingers sought the opening bars of the *Pathetique*. "Why, Margaret plays *beautifully!*" my mother had assured the teacher with the Pekinese. "And she's still just a *child*," my father had said the afternoon Miss Jackson brought the news that although I could still go to Juiliard, I had failed the audition. I wasn't good enough to win the scholarship. "I'm sorry, Mr. Hunter," she'd said, looking Daddy in the eye. "Margaret is talented, your daughter will enjoy the piano all her life, but I'm afraid she simply wasn't born with enough of the necessary *gifts*."

No. I would never make the sounds I could hear by placing a Rubenstein record on my new hi-fi, or by listening to the Horowitz albums my daddy had just given me for my eighteenth birthday. And having learned to love those sounds, I hated my own. I might as well go to Sweet Briar.

I closed the keyboard, gave the piano an affectionate pat on the back, and walked over to Peter's side of the bookshelves. Dear Peter. He hadn't failed the way I'd failed. He'd won his scholarship to Emory. He'd been a brilliant student. A master of English literature.

I tried to remember when Peter had stopped being the young idealist I'd fallen in love with on the beach at Sea Island. Was it the responsibilities of a wife and children that had turned him into the very man he'd said he never wanted to be? A conventional well-heeled lawyer in a well-heeled law firm? A man of Buckhead society wearing gray pin-striped suits? Member of Downtown Rotary, the Carriage Country Club, the Peachtree Golf Club? A man who ate the same brand of cereal every morning, the same bowl of vanilla ice cream every night?

"Never mind," I told the photograph of a man playing Scrabble with his children at the lake. "You've managed to walk the line between convention and individuality far better than your wife has."

Yes. He could laugh when his friends kidded him for his liberal views, for getting up early Sunday mornings to go bird-watching with the local Audubon Club instead of going to church, for still wearing bow ties when he felt like it, for jogging before it became popular, for refusing to attend one more charity ball where the music was too loud for decent conversation or take one more trip to Sea Island where the main activity of the evening was yet another private cocktail party.

In some ways Peter had remained as different from his good old boy buddies as he'd been the first time I met him. But it was easier for a man; a man was a lovable eccentric when he challenged the views of the crowd. A woman, on the other hand, was a pretentious bore. An argumentative bitch.

I studied the other photograph, the one of Peter and me on our honeymoon. It was probably similar to the picture his parents had placed on their mantel: a young married couple looking fearlessly into the camera, with smiles that revealed they thought they had the whole world ahead of them. They were just waiting to make their marks.

"Calm down. Stop exaggerating your miseries," Ida had told me when we were staying in the cottage at Sea Island and I said I might be falling in love with an idealistic law student from Emory. "You'll never have to see that boring boy again," she'd said.

But Peter had arrived unannounced at my parents' front door the day I returned to Atlanta. He'd come, he said, to invite me to join him and some friends who were getting together for lunch downtown.

"What should I wear?" I asked.

"Something casual."

I left him in the den to talk to my mother while I changed into my new flowered-print dress with the kimono sleeves and my new green Capezio flats that matched the color of the trim on the bodice. I didn't know any of Peter's friends. I was afraid they'd think I was too immature for a man like Peter.

"Don't look so worried, Margaret," he said after I'd climbed in the front seat of his dilapidated Plymouth. "They'll think you're terrific. They've probably never seen sleeves on a dress like that before."

He was wearing jeans. His hair was longer than I'd remembered. When he smiled, I had trouble catching my breath.

"I meant to call you," he said, smiling. "I meant to leave you a note," he said, explaining why he'd left Sea Island without one word.

I shrugged and lit a cigarette.

"I have this summer job in Richmond. Did I tell you? I needed to hurry back. And since I knew I'd be coming to Atlanta in two weeks, I figured I could always look you up." He laughed. "So, have you missed me?"

We were stopped at a red light. He reached his arm over the back of the seat and tried to nudge me away from the door handle. He grinned. "Yeah. You missed me."

I couldn't look at him. Why had I let him feel me up on the beach? He probably thought I was a girl who actually *enjoyed* having boys feel her up.

When the light changed, he returned his hands to the steering wheel and began whistling through his teeth.

"So, tell me about this luncheon we're going to, Peter," I said casually, forcing myself to momentarily forget the fact that somehow during that night on the beach I'd accidentally felt him up, too. "Who's going to be there?"

He didn't answer. Instead, he pulled me next to him and kissed the back of my neck. At the next red light he took my cigarette, extinguished it in the ashtray, and began moving his hand down my arm. "You still love me?" he asked, drawing circles in my lap.

I heard a gurgle escape from my mouth.

He laughed again and waited until we'd passed the corner where Mr. Baxter was selling hot pistachio nuts before explaining all I'd need to know about the luncheon at the Lane Rexall Drugstore.

"But I won't know how to act," I said. "I've never been to a sit-in."

"It's easy. You just go limp and let them drag you away without resisting."

He didn't propose to me until I was lying on the floor of a paddy wagon full of other limp and unresisting people.

"Marry the kid," said the large Negro woman whose elbow was killing my back. "He's not much to look at, honey, but he's got busy hands and he won't talk you to death. He sure doesn't seem like the kind of boy who'll turn out to be boring."

No. Despite Ida's initial reaction to him, Peter had never been boring. But when had he stopped being active in unpopular causes and merely started defending them by picking arguments with his friends? I glanced over the titles of the books on his side of the shelves. They were mostly from college and law school days. When had he stopped reading fiction and started reading nothing but nonfiction bestsellers and the newspaper?

The clock in the living room was chiming four-thirty. At least two more hours to go before I could start getting dressed for Buford's party. I wandered back through the empty house, mentally stripping the carpet, waxing the floors, hanging our old drapes on the fashionably bare windows. Then I went upstairs. Annie D. had made up the beds, scrubbed the bathtubs, polished the furniture. The drawers didn't need straightening. It would be three days before I could fix Jimmy another meal.

I lay down on the chaise lounge and opened the book I'd borrowed from Peter's side of the shelves.

Stately, plump Buck Mulligan came from the stairhead, bearing a bowl of lather on which a mirror and razor lay crossed . . .

Yes. After Peter had asked me to marry him, I'd tried to read his favorite book so many times I still knew the opening line by heart. It was always the *next* line that made everybody give up: *"Itroibo ad altare Dei."*

I closed my eyes. Peter wouldn't give a damn if his friends kidded him about his contact lenses or his hair transplant. If people were too stupid to realize how much younger he looked with turquoise eyes and red scratch marks on his scalp, that was their problem, not his. With Peter's gift for rationalization, he could delude himself into believing anything. And what he chose to believe at the moment was that he wasn't forty-six. He was thirty-six.

Our Father who art in heaven.

Had Peter told anyone about how I'd been frigid since Meg's death?

Hallowed be Thy name.

Don't ever let a man touch you *down there*, Grandmother Leticia had warned me. She was tall and thin and wore her long red hair knotted at the back of her neck. Her eyes were the color of bachelor's buttons. You'll go *blind*, she'd said.

And I believe in God the Father Almighty, maker of heaven and earth.

She talked in initials. I never understood her initials, but I knew they were something either very good or very bad. TB and FDR were bad. Whenever she came to stay with Buford and me because Daddy was visiting our mother at the hospital, she'd tuck me into my bed at night and whisper, "Have you had your BM today?"

I had no idea what BM was, but I knew she wanted me to have it. I knew she was proud of me when I whispered, "Yes."

"Good!" she would say. "That's a very good girl, Margaret."

Beatrice would always wait until she heard Grandmother move away from my door before she tiptoed into my room to undo Grandmother's tucking-in. "Do it right," Beatrice would say. And she'd touch my cheek with the back of her dark brown hand and kiss me softly on the forehead. "Sweet dreams, baby," she would tell me.

Beatrice herself had only one dream. She kept it in her basement bedroom inside a knotted brown wool sock. "This here," she'd say, "is Detroit, New York City, Baltimore, and Chicago." I'd watch her untie the knot and reach her hand inside the sock. "This here is Seattle, Washington, D.C., and Boston, Massachusetts."

She'd spill the nickels and dimes and quarters from the sock into the empty bowl that had once been home to three goldfish named Ralph and Louise and Amanda.

"That there," Beatrice would announce, naming her dream, "is living *white*."

"Hush, baby," she crooned the day I went running to the basement to warn her not to ever let a man touch her down there because it would make her blind. "Your grandmama can see all right, can't she? Let it slide on by."

And I believe in Jesus Christ, His only son, who will come to judge the quick and the dead . . .

You'll become insane, Grandmother Leticia had said. And once, when I was nine or ten, we'd gone window-shopping outside of Rich's department store downtown, and she'd said, "Look, Margaret! The mannequins are waving to you!" They were members of the Rich's Teen Board, high school girls from Calvin Academy. Buckhead pinks, I'd heard Buford call them. "Aren't they pretty?" Grandmother asked, her hands darting in and out of her words. "Aren't they just about the prettiest girls you've ever seen?"

Yes. They were modeling Easter dresses. They were posing as still as statues behind the glass.

"Wave back to them," my grandmother urged.

But I was too shy and amazed to wave.

"Well, never mind, dear heart." She took my arm and led me across the street to the bus stop. "Some day when you come to visit me, I'll open the door and find a girl standing there who is prettier by far than any of those girls in that window."

Her apartment had had a bed that pulled down from the wall. A table in the corner with a hot plate on it. A bathtub with lion's paw feet.

"You could die," she'd said. "And it could be even worse than *that*, Margaret. You could end up in a brothel."

And I believe in Jesus Christ, His only son, our Lord. Who was conceived by the Holy Ghost, born of the Virgin Mary, suffered under . . .

"Why?" I asked Mother the night she came into my room to tell me Grandmother Leticia was dead.

"She was tired," Mother answered. "She needed to find a place to rest."

And I believe in all things visible and invisible . . .

Mother lay down beside me on my four-poster bed and waited for me to cry myself to sleep. But I didn't feel like crying. I was trying to remember my grandmother's voice. *Yankee Dudes!* And the way her face smelled of lemon slices when she bent down to tuck me in at night. *They may have attempted to ape the customs of the South, dear heart, but they made a total mockery of it in the process . . .*

After a while I heard Mother ease herself off my bed and close the door softly behind her.

And I believe in the Holy Ghost, the forgiveness of sins, the resurrection of the body, Amen.

I fell asleep, or maybe I did not fall asleep. But sometime during the night I suddenly sat straight up in bed. Someone was in the room. Over by the window, or standing in the corner next to my dollhouse.

"Grandmother?" I whispered.

I lay back on my pillow and waited. Her fireplace had had a mustard-colored heater in it that smelled of sulphur. She wore a locket around her neck that contained a strand of hair from the head of Robert E. Lee.

After a long while, I closed my eyes again and fell into a deep sleep. "Either hair from the head of the general," I thought I heard my father saying in the hallway, "or hair from the tail of the general's horse."

All night long I dreamed of nothing at all, not even of Grandmother Leticia. But as I slept, I knew that death had changed her body into the feeling that was tucking the blankets around me. Had changed her voice into a feeling that could speak without words: *There, Margaret,* she was saying to me as I slept. *There, there, dear heart.*

"Why did she die?" Meg asked when she was so small she had to climb up on a box to reach the old four-poster bed I'd given her. We were kneeling beside the bed so I could hear her prayers, so her Great-grandmother Leticia in heaven could hear her prayers.

"She wanted to go to heaven so she could be with my Grandfather Buford," I said. Gone to heaven, I didn't try to explain, because a Mr. Hampton married her soon after she became widowed and took all her money and ran away to Arizona. Left her with two little children to raise all by herself. Left her with nothing but shame and debts and whispers behind her back.

"Your mother would have died in the poorhouse if it hadn't been for me!" Daddy yelled at Mother after Grandmother Leticia had climbed the steps of the old downtown library and climbed a ladder to the roof and jumped from the ledge into the arms of a shoe salesman from Chicago.

"Settle out of court, Walter," Mother begged. "Please, Walter. We don't want the neighbors to know."

But Daddy was not in a mood to settle anything. "I paid for that woman's rent and bought her clothes and put food in her mouth. Gave her everything she owned. Nobody gets one more red cent from me because of your lah-de-dah mother!" Daddy kept yelling after the salesman sued from the grave on behalf of his wife, Mrs. Henry Gilbert, and his unborn son, Gilly Gilbert. ("He's the size of a pea," Buford had said. "He's inside Mrs. Gilbert's vagina, and he's no bigger than a lima bean.")

"Walter! Your children will never be able to live this down if you don't settle out of court!"

"She should have thought of that before she jumped," Daddy said. "She never wanted you to marry me. Do you remember that, Charlotte? Your fancy, highfalutin socialite mother never thought I was good enough for you," Daddy had said the night I tiptoed into Mother's room and found her crying at her vanity table, whispering "I hate you, Walter Hunter" into the mirror.

Thy kingdom come, Thy will be done.

"There, there, Margaret," Grandmother Leticia murmured in

my dreams while I lay on the chaise lounge with a book open in my lap. "It has nothing to do with *you*, dear heart. Peter is out of his mind. Why, he doesn't even know how old he is! The only explanation is a brain tumor."

"Poor Peter," Mother wailed in my dreams. "He has a *brain* tumor!"

"Hush, baby," Beatrice crooned. "Let it slide on by."

"Hah," Buford said, smirking at me from behind Beatrice's rocking chair. "It's the size of a pea," he whispered meanly. "Peter's tumor is no bigger than a lima bean."

8

I was awakened by Ida shaking my shoulders and ordering me to get up. "What are you thinking of?" she said. "It's almost seven o'clock. If I hadn't come over here to borrow some of your silver for the garden club meeting tomorrow, you would have slept right through your brother's party."

I felt drugged. Exhausted. "I've changed my mind," I said. My feet groped for the rug. "To tell you the truth, Ida, I'm not all that sure he really invited me. It was more like he told Mother he *meant* to invite me."

"Fix your hair, Margaret. Where are your electric rollers?"

"Getting an invitation from your mother is not quite the same thing." I brushed past Ida and headed into the bathroom to do away with myself. Razor blades. Sleeping pills. An overdose of Peter's vitamins.

"And you need to put some Erase under your eyes," Ida said, following behind me. "If you don't go to that party after making me listen to you complain about having Babs to your family Thanksgiving dinner for the past twenty years when you've never even set foot inside her house, I swear I'm never going to speak to you again."

Ida's threat seemed unlikely. I ignored her and began moving things around in the medicine cabinet. But apparently Peter had taken everything except my douche powder. I couldn't imagine how you could kill yourself with that unless you mixed it with cyanide and drank it.

"Think of all the interesting new people you can meet," Ida said. "Babs is bound to know some attractive men."

"I don't want to meet any more interesting new people. I can't think of anything I'd less like to do at the moment than meet an attractive man. I'm not feeling all that friendly toward the interesting, attractive men I've already met."

"If you're talking about Peter, you can forget it. I hate to say I told you so, but I told you the first time you laid eyes on that boy he was going to end up dull and ugly."

"Oh, Ida. Please shut up."

"Okay. Peter is fascinating. Handsome. He's just going through delayed adolescence." She came up behind me and looked at me through the mirror on the medicine cabinet. She put her arm around my waist. "I'm sorry," she said quietly.

I pulled away from her. *Don't pity me. I have more than enough pity for us both.*

"So! What are we planning to wear?" she asked in her cheery Tinkerbell voice.

"I'm not going."

But Ida was no longer behind me. When I returned to the bedroom, she was standing with her back to me, rummaging through my closet. "This is sweet," she said over her shoulder. She pulled out a dress I'd forgotten I had. I'd bought it at Laura Ashley's at the same time I got the pioneer skirt and blouse to wear downtown to see Peter.

"Put this on," she ordered, holding it up to me. "And then get the hell out of this depressing house and go show Buford's intellectual friends just who you are. They've probably never met a Buckhead pink before. They'll find you charming."

I smiled. "Ida, what on earth would I do without you?"

"Exactly. That's what I've been trying to tell you all these years. Now you march right into that party and then you come back and tell me what a famous spiritualist looks like. I can't imagine!"

I walked over to the mirror. The dress was pink with little flowers on it. It had a white Peter Pan collar, a sash at the waist. "I don't know, Ida. You're sure it's not *too* sweet?"

"It's perfect. Trust me. It's absolutely *perfect*."

"Honestly, Harold," I'd told my yardman the day I learned from Mother about the spiritualist moving next door to my brother and his wife. "The last thing on earth I want to do is crash Buford's little party."

"Yes, ma'am." He'd handed me my gardening gloves. "Don't see much of Mr. Buford no more. Used to be short for his age when he was young. Now he got more of your daddy's looks, don't he? Big, heavyset fellow. Uh-huh. Seen him that week Meg passed away. Got that bald head and them bushy red eyebrows. Ain't nothing better than family when you feeling low, Miz Margaret. Only family I got left is Earllovette, and she just be a wife. Ain't like she be blood."

"Yes, but my brother may not like me all that much, Harold."

"Why, everybody likes you, Miz Margaret! Maybe he just be mad at you a while."

"It's been a long while. Sometimes I think he's been angry at me ever since I was born and forced him to give up his status as the only child. Or maybe Beatrice was right: he resented the roles our parents assigned us. 'Big brother supposed to act his age,' she'd mutter whenever Daddy spanked him for being mean to me. 'I reckon you think baby sister's too young to know any better, Mr. Hunter?'"

"Uh-huh. I remember Beatrice. Tall, thin lady with a temper. She be always chewing starch. Remember when I used to let you and her ride in my bakery wagon?"

"Yes. I do remember, Harold."

"Lord, you was a spunky thing back then, sure enough!" Harold said, chuckling.

"Was I?" His remark surprised me. I would have thought he'd

have said Buford was the spunky one. But maybe that wasn't until we were older. And it occurred to me as Harold began talking about Jasmine, the horse that had pulled his wagon, that perhaps my brother's grudge against me didn't begin until we were in our teens, until that morning at the breakfast table when Daddy lit a Pall Mall, dropped the match on his plate of scrambled eggs, and said to Buford: "It's about time you started being more like your sister sitting over there. You don't see Margaret being disrespectful to her father. Margaret will be respectful to her father for the rest of her life."

Daddy was furious with Buford because when Buford was four he'd stolen a Baby Ruth candy bar from Mr. Levine's fruit emporium. When he was nine, he'd lost a perfectly good sweater one day when he was playing in the park. When he was thirteen, he'd been given a guitar for Christmas and had never practiced it. "You never catch Margaret not practicing her piano!" Daddy said.

No! Unlike some people at the breakfast table Daddy could mention, Buford's little sister had not lost interest the minute her daddy gave her a musical instrument.

"Never mind, dear," Mother said. "Go ahead with your reading, Walter. We're extremely engrossed."

Daddy had discovered his old prewar copy of *How to Win Friends and Influence People* in a box of junk Mother was giving away to the Salvation Army. Although the edition of his favorite book was somewhat outdated, he now saw it as an opportunity to once again try to teach his ungrateful son a bit of sound, common sense.

" 'I was walking up the stairs of the Long Island station in New York . . .' " he began reading.

Mother nodded encouragement. I looked down quickly at my plate. Daddy was reading in a strange radiolike voice I'd never heard him use before, a kind of imitation of Edward R. Murrow.

"Excuse me, Daddy," Buford said, interrupting the reading. "But by New York do you mean New York *City*?"

"Of course I mean New York City!" Daddy looked around the

table angrily. "Does anybody know of any New York besides New York *City*?"

And Daddy was furious with Buford because when Buford was sixteen he'd taken a date to dinner at the Carriage Country Club and ordered Chateaubriand. Did everybody remember that? How Buford had ordered the most expensive meal on the menu, even though you could bet your life Mr. Buford sitting over there looking so smug didn't pay for that dinner. No! The person who'd had to dig in his pocket to pay for Chateaubriand was the same person who'd had to pay for everything else Mr. Buford took for granted. A roof over his head! Food on the table! The shirts on his back! A brand new 1955 automobile for his eighteenth birthday! The Hunter Baking Company on a silver platter!

Ah, well. The Hunter Baking Company on a silver platter. And Daddy was furious with Buford because he'd just informed the family that he didn't *want* to spend the rest of his life at the Hunter Baking Company. No, indeed! Mr. Buford sitting there looking so psychic at the breakfast table wanted to become a freak! Did everybody understand what Margaret's brother had just announced? That he'd been scheming behind his father's back, and he wasn't returning to Georgia Tech in the fall, where his father had graduated from college and his grandfather had graduated from college? No. Georgia Tech wasn't good enough for Margaret's brother. Margaret's brother was going to transfer to Duke University where some nutty kook was pulling the wool over Atheistic Communistic eyes by doing experiments he called ESP. "If God had wanted people to have ESP," Daddy informed us, "He would have given it to them and told them about it in the *Book of Revelations!*"

And if Buford ever expected to work for the Hunter Baking Company, he'd better start finding out that life was not a game of guessing symbols on the backs of cue cards. Life was hard work. Did everybody at the table remember how Buford Hunter had never known the meaning of W-O-R-K? How Buford Hunter had never appreciated the meaning of M-O-N-E-Y?

"Margaret," Daddy said, lighting up another Pall Mall and glaring across the table at Buford, "tell your psychic brother over there what Mister Carnegie means when he says New York."

"He means New York City."

"Now, Walter," Mother said. "Calm down and finish your little story. You don't want to upset your ulcer."

" 'I was walking up the stairs of the Long Island station in . . .' "

Daddy paused, daring anyone to make another interruption.

"That's right, dear," Mother said. "In New York. Go on, Walter."

He nodded, satisfied, and slipped back into his Edward R. Murrow voice. " 'Directly in front of me thirty or forty crippled boys on canes and crutches were struggling up the stairs . . .' "

I didn't look at Buford while our father related how one of the little lads Mister Carnegie had seen on those stairs had been so crippled he'd had to be carried. And how Mister Carnegie had been so astonished when he saw that the poor little lad was nonetheless jolly and gay, he had naturally walked right over to the man in charge to ask him to explain: " 'When a boy realizes he is going to be a cripple for the rest of his life, he is shocked at first; but, after he gets over the shock,' " Daddy intoned, " 'he usually resigns himself to his fate and then becomes happier than normal boys.' "

"Ha!" Buford laughed. He got up from his chair and slapped Daddy on the back to let him see how happy he'd become. "Ha! Ha! Ha! Ha! Ha!" Buford laughed, leaving the table to go to his room and to pack his clothes and to leave Mother a note on her vanity table mirror that informed us he was not coming home until he'd made a million dollars to cram up his father's nose. "Ha!" he wrote the morning he ran away to make a bundle as a migrant worker on a farm in Texas, and as a migrant worker on an avocado plantation in California, and as the future son-in-law of the owner not only of that avocado plantation but also the fifth largest phamaceutical company in the world.

"Ha! Ha! Ha!" he laughed, watching my surprise and my joy

when he reappeared, unannounced, at my wedding reception almost four years later.

Peter liked this grown man with long red hair and a beard and a great big honest-to-goodness smile the minute he met him. "He's the kind of man," Peter said, "who seems to know what he wants to do."

One of the things Buford wanted to do that night at our wedding reception was to tell Peter and me about the woman he'd brought with him. She was a published novelist and looked "old enough," Ida whispered just before I tossed her my bridal bouquet, "to be her own mother!"

"You'll love Babs," Buford said, putting his arm around me. "She's got brains and talent," he said. "And maturity."

"Huh," Daddy said.

"And she's got three million dollars," Buford added.

Daddy looked across the ballroom and gave this Babs person a second reading.

"Enough money," Buford said to Peter and me later in the evening, "to be able to tell Dad what he can do with his Presbyterian work ethic. Enough money to keep me out of that goddamned baking company forever and ever, amen."

"So why are you still mad at me?" I practiced asking my brother on the way to his party. "See how everything always works out fine in the end?"

———

Inman Park, where Buford and Babs live, is Atlanta's oldest official subdivision. When it was developed around the turn of the century, it was only a three-mile trolley ride away from the heart of downtown. Many of Atlanta's leading businessmen and society matrons made their homes there in Victorian mansions and Colonial-style townhouses that were protected from their neighbors by wrought-iron fences and statues of Negro jockeys guarding wrought-iron gates.

I hadn't been to Inman Park in years, but I discovered most

of the houses and fences and jockeys I'd known as a child still existed. The only difference was that the faces of the latter were now painted over with white enamel.

From the outside, my brother's house reminded me of a red brick castle. It had minarets and domes and a front porch as wide as a moat. I thought it might be Romanesque, but when I walked inside I found Babs in the drawing room explaining to a dozen or so guests that actually it was a style she and Buford called "Masculine." From the way her eyebrows were raised when she said this word, I guessed that she was trying to imply just how much fun a girl who writes romance novels about small-town women from the South emerging into full sexuality could have in such a male abode. When she saw me standing in the doorway, she looked surprised.

I felt embarrassed. I shouldn't have arrived at her party wearing the wrong clothes. If I had known any of her other guests, I would have called them beforehand and learned I was supposed to have arrived in something hand-woven, something draped from my shoulders with feathers or beads. Instead of poking tacky little pearl buttons in my ears, I should have hung loops the size of vacuum cleaner fan belts.

I turned away from Babs and began wandering through the house looking for Buford. I counted seventeen fireplaces in seventeen rooms. One of the Little Girls rooms was decorated in a literary motif. The pictures on the walls were photographs of famous authoresses, and the toilet paper was imprinted with excerpts from *The Book of Lists*. The excerpt I read was entitled "Twenty-one Best-known Stuffed or Embalmed Humans or Animals in the History of the World." It explained how Juan Peron had embalmed Eva's body and was planning to build a mausoleum to put it in, but then he was suddenly forced into exile and the body disappeared. Nobody knew where it was for almost twenty years, not until a friend who dined with Peron admitted to somebody that the body was now present every evening at the dinner table along with Juan and his new wife, Isabel.

I slipped the roll of toilet paper into my pocketbook, and as I headed back downstairs to look for Buford some more I tried to visualize the scene with Peter and me instead of with Juan and Eva. It would take place in our dining room, of course. I'd be at the foot of the table, probably. Peter would have to tie my body to the chair in several places: around the waist, under the armpits. And he'd need to tape my eyelids open—what would be the point of my being there if I couldn't see how much Sydney enjoyed my company? But Peter could do these things easily. He was a divorce lawyer; he knew every little trick.

I was about to enter the parlor again when I spotted an open door that led down to the basement. I decided to see if what Buford had told me at one of my Thanksgiving dinners was true. Supposedly, in a crawl space directly beneath the parlor, there was a 1902 White Steamer automobile that had belonged to the man who'd built the house over and around it without remembering to leave a way to get it out. I saw it at the same moment I heard Buford begin to explain the details to his neighbors. "The Death Car of Montague Strange," he was saying as I came down the steps. "His ghost still roams the premises at night. Babs and I like to think he's the most charming feature of Inman Park."

I didn't know. To tell the truth, I wasn't having much fun at the party. The prominent businessmen and society matrons of Inman Park's past had been replaced by important artists and musicians and writers and actors and professional visionaries. They didn't like me any more than my host and hostess liked me. What was I supposed to say to such people? Every time I mustered the nerve to introduce myself, they answered with something like: "Mrs. Peter Bridges? Now, tell us. Just what does a Mrs. Peter Bridges *do*?"

I was tired of trying to carry on conversations with Buford's intellectual friends. A glass blower had actually flicked her fingernail in my face when I told her that what a Mrs. Peter Bridges *used* to do was work at the Nearly New. When I'd explained to an architect that I had the ability to dream concurrent dreams, she'd pretended to remove a speck of sleep from her eye and then had turned her back on me.

As soon as Buford saw me standing on the basement steps, he gave me the kind of phony smile a man gives his kid sister when he's not sure what she's doing there, and then he said, "Hi."

"Hi," I answered. Then I turned around and headed back upstairs to the dining room. I was suddenly too depressed to care whether or not my brother thought I was rude. I was going to eat and run. A Southern Belle Magnolia Honkie Buckhead Pink belonged on the other side of town from Buford and Babs.

In the dining room, however, all I found to eat were potato chip dips, assorted cheeses, and bowls of trail mix. While I nibbled a raisin I cheered myself up by comparing my abilities as a hostess to those of my sister-in-law. I remembered the last party Peter and I had given. It had been in our old house in Buckhead, on the night of the garden club's 1980 Spring Bazaar.

"Everyone absolutely *raved* about my menu," I informed a musky-odored man standing next to me. "All the recipes were from Junior League cookbooks: Mrs. More of Nashville's *Baked Apples filled with Spiked Sweet Potatoes*, Mrs. Gamble of Charleston's *New Cut Plantation String Beans . . .* "

He moved to the other side of the table and began spreading Roquefort on a Ritz cracker.

"Also, Mrs. McMurphy of Mobile's *Garden Crisp Salad*," I told Babs when she walked up to me. "And, of course, Mrs. Bridges of Atlanta's *Lemon Butter Chicken Breasts*."

"Well, you know how *I* am!" Babs said with a laugh.

No. I had no idea how she was. I didn't know her that well.

"If I cooked," she said, moving toward the front hallway to greet another guest, "I'd never find time to do everything else."

Yes, I thought, watching her go. As soon as she left the hallway, I'd sneak back to Arcadia Heights. I remembered that somewhere in Minevah's library table in the living room were the pictures Jimmy had taken of my dinner party: Mary Earle sitting on our den sofa with her head on Wally's shoulder, Ida and Georgina Watkins kneeling in the middle of our kitchen floor playing some kind of game, Peter waving one of Mrs. Shaw of Tampa's *Mother Carrie's English Tea Muffins* in Cynthia Foster's face. There was this one picture I particularly liked of twenty or so guests walking past the card tables filled with bazaar items that had not quite sold yet—Patsy Pierson's lime-green burlap "Garden Rake Coverlet," several of Bootsey Kelley's mousetraps decorated to look like napkin holders, my own lavender and pink crocheted afghan.

Somewhere among those pictures were the ones Jimmy had taken when he came upstairs that night and caught Ida and Mary Earle and me sprawled on top of Meg's four-poster bed, listening to her read an article from an old *W* that Joyce Belinda had accidentally left at the house when she delivered her bazaar items the day before.

"Entertaining IN Style," Meg said, giving us the title of the article.

She was wearing a Wellesley nightshirt brought home from a visit to the college she was going to enter in the fall. She was sitting cross-legged on the bed, the article in her lap, and Jimmy's photograph had captured the exact moment when Ida and I leaned toward Meg and hugged her in laughter at all the things she was reading out loud to prove that her mother's entertaining style was definitely OUT.

"According to one of the most fabulously exciting hostesses in the world," Meg informed us, "it is IN to serve cocktails for precisely forty-five minutes and then serve dinner *promptly* at nine. Never wait for *anyone,* not even the Queen."

My own dinner had been served a bit late. It was after one in the morning when Jimmy took that picture. Meg was happy. Her finger was tracing a line across the page.

"And listen to this, Mom! She says the parties given by her good friend the Duchess of Windsor are always *marvelously* presented and she laments the fact that there is a certain game that cannot be had in the United States unless one goes out and shoots it oneself . . ."

"Who laments that?" I asked. I was holding one of Mary Earle's unsold bazaar items above my head: a long tube of calico filled with twenty pounds of sand. Mary Earle had explained it was an old-fashioned draft dodger, something to put on a windowsill to ward off winter chills. "The fabulously exciting hostess?" I asked, trying to drape the tube around Ida's shoulders like a boa, "or her good friend the Duchess?"

Yes. We had all been extremely happy. Old friends are the best friends. Strangers are the worst.

I stood in my sister-in-law's dining room and waited for the woman with the vacuum cleaner fan belt earrings to turn her back so I could hide my olive pit in the bowl of trail mix. Then I looked around for Buford to tell him good-bye.

"It's been lovely," I said. "Absolutely lovely."

But he may not have heard me. He was in the next room having a conversation with a man I suddenly realized I knew extremely well. He was the actor from the Academy Theater who had shown Peter and me one night in *The Glass Menagerie* just how miraculous—how heartbreaking—life could be. Oh, we had seen him on stage many, many times. And there he was, not forty feet away from me, in my own brother's house!

I began rehearsing opening lines: "How do you do? I've been meaning for the longest time to drop you a little note to tell you how much I love you." I began walking toward him. "Good evening. You don't know me, but I think about you all the time." I was *striding* toward him.

He saw me coming. Panic was written all over his face. What was he supposed to do with this thin middle-aged matron bearing down on him with a stupid smile? With an arm stretched out in front of her as though she thought she could shake his hand from twenty feet away?

I stopped. I'd seen this man cry in *Death of a Salesman*. I'd seen him kill a woman in *Of Mice and Men*.

I turned around. One awful night I'd seen him in some modern play when he'd actually lowered his trousers and exposed his naked buttocks to me.

No. I opened the front door and fled from this man. I was on the sidewalk, approaching my car, before I realized that my arm was still extended.

OTHER THINGS I MEANT TO DO

Tell Buford that he and his wife are the least charming features of Inman Park.

9

The minute I pulled into my driveway I knew something terrible must have happened while I was off at the party. Jimmy wasn't supposed to be back until Sunday, but every light in the house was on. I started calling to him before I even got the back door open. His father had probably been bitten by a water moccasin—I'd warned him a million times—or he'd been run over by some drunken kid speeding in a motorboat.

"Jimmy?"

I ran through the kitchen and found him slumped over the breakfast room table with his face buried in his fists. "What's the matter?" I asked. His father had *drowned.* "Quick! Answer me!"

He looked up at me and shrugged. "Nothing," he said, listlessly. "Why do you always think something has to be the matter?"

I sat down opposite him. He must have had a terrible argument with his father. Said things he'd be too proud to repeat to me. ("Come on, Dad. Apologize to Mom so everything will be all right again.")

Jimmy pushed his chair away from the table and walked into the kitchen.

I followed him. "Talk to me," I said. "Where's your dad?"

"Aw, Mom."

I peered over his shoulder into the refrigerator. I could grill a steak. Mash a potato. String some green beans.

"I'm not hungry, Mom. I just want something to drink."

Iced tea. I could borrow a lemon from old Mrs. Ferguson next door.

"Forget it. This Coke's okay."

"Well?" I trailed him back to the breakfast room. "Are you just going to stand there? What happened at the lake between you and your father?"

"Nothing, I told you." He flipped his chair around and straddled it with his arms resting over the ladder-back. Macho man. Good old boy. His father's son.

"Then why did he bring you home early?"

"He got a call from some client who needed him. It sounded like an emergency, so we came back. He's picking me up again tomorrow night after work. It's no big deal."

"Of *course* it's a big deal. This was supposed to be your spring break. If he had to bring you home, he could at least have promised to pick you up again early in the morning so you'd have the entire day up there."

"Don't worry about it." He took a swig of his drink and began grinning to himself.

"What?" I asked.

"It was kind of funny, Mom," he said, still grinning. "She was real hysterical."

"*Who* was hysterical?"

"The client I just told you about. Sydney something. Apparently somebody broke into her apartment while she was at work, and she was scared to stay by herself. She wanted Dad to be there when the police arrived."

"Oh, yeah?"

Jimmy laughed. "The police think whoever the guy was must have been on drugs. The only things he stole were some stupid classical record albums, but he shortsheeted her bed and he used one of her lipsticks to write a note on the bathroom mirror that said, 'Hardings was here!' Sydney swore she'd never heard of anyone named Hardings in her life, but I don't think Dad believed her."

I walked over to the table and sank slowly into my chair. I stared at Jimmy. It was unforgivable of Peter to introduce an adulteress to his own son.

"Whoever he was," Jimmy said, "he went through her desk and rearranged her canceled checks for the past year according to categories. You know? Like all the rent checks were in one pile and all credit card bills in another. The guy even alphabetized the ones to different department stores. It was crazy."

"Yes."

"And he used the dishwasher to Clorox the hell out of one of her nightgowns."

I raised my head from the table. "And?"

"And what?"

"And what else happened? That's it? You went over there with your dad, you met this crazy client, you waited for the police, and then what?"

"Nothing." He swigged down the rest of his Coca-Cola, crushed the can, and tossed it one-handed over his shoulder into the wastebasket. "I'm bushed, Mom. I'm going to bed."

"Well, it's not fair. Your father should have taken you back to the lake."

Another shrug. "We're only missing the one day. Dad said he'd make it up to me later."

"What else did he say?"

"Nothing." He stretched his arms over his head. "Oh, yeah," he said, cracking his knuckles. "I forgot. He told me to tell you the bottom line isn't you, it's him."

"What's that supposed to mean?"

"I don't know, but he thought it was pretty funny. He laughed when he said it. 'Tell your mother it's fine with me if she wants to become a bag lady,' he said, 'but she's under no legal obligation to do so.'"

"Oh."

I was trying to decide what Peter's purpose was in sending me such a message through our son—was I supposed to feel stupid? Grateful? Relieved?—when Jimmy suddenly stood up, yawned, and flipped his chair around to face the table.

"Well, that's very fair of your father," I said, bitterly. "Now that he's proved how fair he is, I guess I'm supposed to feel guilty."

Jimmy didn't answer. I watched him leave the room and head toward the stairs. Cool. Casual. With just enough of a swagger to make me want to beat my fists on the back of his camouflage shirt.

I lay my head on the table and waited until I heard his door slam shut. Then I got up and began wandering through the house turning off lights. In the living room, I noticed through the window that several cars were parked along the street in front of the Matthews's house. Ah, well. Ida was having a party and she hadn't invited me.

"Never mind," I'd tell her when I called her in the morning. "I don't blame you." No. Women always enjoyed having an extra man at the table, but as long as I remained a divorcee, I'd probably never be invited to another party in my life.

I had turned on the burglar alarm in Peter's study and was half-way up the stairs before it occurred to me that what I *could* blame Ida for was the fact that now I wouldn't be able to get to the garden club meeting. If she hadn't persuaded me to break into Sydney's apartment, Peter wouldn't have screwed up Jimmy's first day of vacation by bringing him back from the lake and I wouldn't be having to spend tomorrow making it up to him by taking him out to lunch and to a movie.

I knocked lightly on Jimmy's door, suddenly remembering that we never ate lunch at the same kinds of places anymore. And the only movie I wanted to see at the moment was a woman's movie: *An Affair to Remember.*

His room was dark. My son with no problems—why do you always think something has to be the matter, Mom?—was already asleep. I tiptoed over to his bed and listened for a moment to his easy breathing. Yes, I thought, tucking the sheet around him. His sister and I had always loved *An Affair to Remember*. We'd watched it on television together dozens of times.

"Sentimental garbage," Jimmy and Peter called it, sneering at Meg and me whenever they walked through the den and caught us crying at the sight of Cary Grant standing in the doorway of Deborah Kerr's apartment about to say farewell forever.

"Shhh!" Meg would beg over her shoulder. "This is our favorite scene."

It was Christmas Eve and Cary had dropped by unexpectedly to bring Deborah a gift of a shawl that had once belonged to his dead grandmother. He hadn't seen Deborah in almost a year, not since the day she'd promised to give him time to change his life so they could get married. If he stopped being an idle playboy living off rich women and became, instead, the great artist she knew he was born to be, in exactly six months she would meet him at noon at the top of the Empire State Building. "The nearest place to heaven," she'd said, "because *you'll* be there!"

Oh, Cary loved Deborah so! He had kept their date. He had waited for her all day and all night in a thunderstorm. And now, as he paused in the doorway trying to find the strength to leave, he knew he would never see her again.

Deborah watched him turn away, hesitate, and then turn back to give her one last look of yearning. Oh, he didn't realize she loved him too! He had no idea that the reason she was lying so still on the sofa was because on the way to meet him that day her legs had been run over by a truck. No! She loved him too much to ever tie him down to marriage with a cripple.

"You know," Cary said, his voice choking with emotion, "I painted a portrait of you with that shawl around your shoulders the way it is tonight. I never thought I could part with it, but the gallery owner told me a woman in a wheelchair rolled in one day and saw in it what I'd hoped *you* would have seen in it one day, and so I . . ."

A horrible thought brushed against him. His dimple quivered.

"And so, I thought why not just give it to her?"

He walked slowly back into the room.

"The gallery owner said she was too poor to buy it, and . . ."

He passed the sofa.

"And, anyway, I could never take money for it . . ."

He placed his hand on the knob of Deborah's bedroom door. "And . . ."

For one heartbreaking moment, he closed his eyes. Then, gathering his courage, he opened the door. There, reflected in the mirror above her bed, was his painting of the woman he adored!

Meg and I knew the next lines by heart. "Oh, my dear and darling!" we groaned along with Cary.

He rushed over to the sofa, buried his face in Deborah's arms.

"Don't cry, dearest," Meg and Deborah told him.

"How can you watch such sentimental garbage?"

"Shhhh." We grabbed another Kleenex.

"If you can learn to paint," I assured Cary, "I can learn to walk."

"Yes!" Meg cried. "Anything is possible, darling. Don't you think?"

"But, oh!" I sobbed. "If something terrible had to happen to one of us, why *did* it have to be *you*?"

Jimmy threw himself off the bed with a howl. "For crying out loud, Mom! What in the hell do you think you're doing?"

"I'm sorry."

"That's disgusting!" He stared down at his sheet. "You blew your nose! What kind of a mother sneaks up on somebody when he's asleep and blows her nose on his sheet?"

"No, you don't understand, Jimmy. I forgot where I was for a minute. It was an accident." I reached out to hug him. "Honestly, darling, I—"

"Jesus! Leave me alone!" He stormed out of the room wearing nothing but his khaki jockey shorts.

"Wait!" I called, chasing him down the stairs. "Let me explain!"

He didn't answer. He was headed toward the basement. He was stumbling down the steps, jerking open the door to the darkroom, locking it in my face.

———

"I could kill you, Ida."

She sighed into the phone. "We have dinner guests, Margaret, potential clients. I can't talk. I'll call you back in the morning."

"It was all your fault," I said.

Another sigh. "*What* was all my fault?"

"You should never have made me go to Buford's party. It was a terrible party. I made a complete ass of myself. I looked like something out of *Little House on the Prairie*. Everybody else there was arty and intellectual. I told you I wouldn't belong."

"I'm sure they thought you were charming. I've got to hang up now. Arnold's showing slides of that Queen Anne on Demeter Drive he can't get rid of. Fix yourself a cup of Sleepy Time tea, take a Valium, and get in the bed, Margaret. You're just tired."

"I'm already in the bed."

"Well, then go to sleep."

"You told me to let you know what a famous spiritualist looks like."

"All right. Hurry up and tell me."

"Fat. Foreign. Female."

"Good."

"But I don't want to talk about Buford's party. I want to talk about the party Peter and I gave last year after the garden club bazaar. Remember? That was the best party I've ever been to."

"Come off of it, Margaret. It was a total disaster. That party was so bad you've never had another one."

"No. Remember how you and Mary Earle and I ended up in Meg's room listening to her read from *W* about famous hostesses? She was so funny that night! She was wearing the nightshirt I bought her when we visited Wellesley, and she said there was this one hostess who always dressed for her dining room? Who would only buy her designer gowns in colors compatible with her wallpaper?"

"What I remember was you forgot to turn off your oven and Georgina Watkins and I had to spend half the night on your kitchen floor trying to scrape black crap from the chicken. All the guests were drunk out of their minds by the time we finally got the food on the table. And Jimmy was making a complete nuisance of himself poking that camera of his into everybody's face."

"And another hostess said she always wore Magriffe eau de cologne? *Never*, she said, any kind of 'allergy-activating perfume.'"

"Is this why you called me? To go over some old article in *W*? I don't understand how you could have forgotten that party, Margaret. You and Joyce Belinda had a fight about those stupid draft dodgers Mary Earle made for the bazaar—you kept making fun of her by trying to drape one around her neck—and Peter got so furious with Cynthia Foster when she started spouting off about how everybody hates lawyers that he crammed an English muffin down her throat. Trust me, it was a terrible party. And we had to help Mary Earle throw up in your toilet, and she kept moaning she was dying, and you kept laughing until she told us she had inflammatory breast cancer. I'll *never* forget that party! It was the worst party of my entire life."

"You're only remembering the bad parts."

"Go to bed, Margaret. It's late. I've got to entertain Arnold's clients and I've got to get up early tomorrow to help Harold arrange the lawn chairs for the meeting."

"The trouble with you, Ida," I said, "is you never see the good side of things. We were extremely happy that night. Somewhere in this house I've got the pictures Jimmy took of you and Mary Earle and me on Meg's bed."

"I'm hanging up."

"Meg was beautiful that night. Remember? She had her hair piled on top of her head, and she was wearing her new nightshirt, and she was so young and full of herself everybody wanted to hug her."

"Good night, Margaret. Sweet dreams."

Yes. I'd remember that night as long as I lived. We had laughed and hugged. We'd had no idea that the next day Meg would be dead.

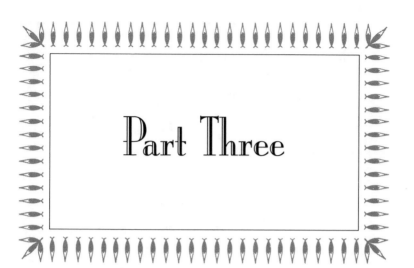

Part Three

6 P.M. Harold and I are still on Ida's roof.

The men are returning from the city. I watch their cars pull off the highway and drive slowly through the streets of Arcadia Heights.

Two children on Big Wheels are down at the intersection, examining the scene of the accident this afternoon. When they spot a black Mercedes turning onto Aphrodite, they begin pedaling madly down the sidewalk, racing it home.

On Hercules, the president of First United Savings and Loan has stopped at the bottom of his driveway to retrieve the evening paper from under the lawn sprinkler where Mrs. Ferguson's grandchild, Billy, tossed it a few minutes ago.

I scan Demeter Drive until I come to the Georgian house at the corner. A man in a business suit is sitting on his front veranda playing jacks with a little girl wearing a bright yellow sundress. The scene reminds me of when my Daddy used to come home from work and sometimes join me in a game of mumbley-peg or toy cars before he went inside to see Mother and Buford.

"Why?" his confused eyes seem to ask me now. He stares up at me from his red leather armchair in the den. "How did it happen?" his mouth, silent since his stroke last spring, seems to want to say. "Is man predestined to end up as helpless as he began?"

The little girl drops her jacks, one at a time, into her father's briefcase. He waits for her to lock it, then holds the front door open for her and sweeps her ahead of him into the house with a gallant wave of his hand.

Arnold arrived home fifteen minutes ago. He hasn't a clue we're on his roof. He parked next to the patio, walked past the stacks of folded lawn chairs, and went inside to change into his jogging outfit. Now he is three blocks away, watching Ida and her girlfriends play their little tennis match.

Little Arnold is gone too. He followed his dad out of the house, threw some camping gear into the back of his van, and drove off. Harold and I took advantage of the empty house by sneaking down the ladder, piece by piece, to use the bathroom facilities. While I searched through Ida's kitchen drawers for a flashlight to have in case it gets dark before I finish my journal, Harold went to the toolshed to bring up a couple of pairs of garden gloves. He may be finding it a tad boring to watch me writing my memoirs. Since we returned to the roof, he's been cleaning out the gutters.

"Sure do stink, don't it?" he says, scooping out a mass of wet leaves and God knows what. He plops it down beside him on the cedar shingles.

The roof is huge, a vast landscape of craggy hills and shallow valleys. The gutters are like a narrow river surrounding it, polluting the air with the odor of decay.

I begin patting my own handful of gunk into a mud pie. I try to prick the top with a twig, the way I used to do as a child playing house on the bank of the creek, but the twig breaks. "Oh, to hell with it," I say. I'm ready for the day to end, for darkness to hide the sight of a mother falling out of the range of her son's camera. I take off my gloves and throw them to Harold. Then I crawl back up the roof to the chimney.

MORE OBSERVATIONS

1. *When you accidentally drop a beetle on its back, it flips in the air with a* click! *and then lands right side up again.*
2. *A crabapple blossom may smell sweet, but its taste is bitter.*

*3. A gutter in springtime contains dead leaves. Also catkins
and maple seeds and acorns. Dogwood blossoms. Mimosa
fronds and pine cones and lichen. Puffballs. Spider webs.
Bird feathers. At the very bottom, eating its way through a
thick red-clay slime, is something that is either a swarm of
termites or a swarm of flying ants.*

"Ants," Harold says, flopping down beside me. He has removed
his gloves, and he begins slapping them softly against his knee.
"You say they find another body this morning?" he murmurs,
returning to the subject we were discussing before he saw our
chance to get into Ida's house. "Don't seem hardly likely, Miz
Margaret."

"No . . ." I wish I'd never brought up the news program
Annie D. was watching in the kitchen when I went downstairs
to tell her I was leaving for the garden club meeting. Harold
wouldn't begin to understand why I've become obsessed with the
missing and murdered children case. Why I study the pictures
of grieving mothers in the newspapers, watch them being interviewed on television, feel their anguish, know the sudden blank-
ness that falls over their faces. What I can never explain to Harold
is my need to touch the justice of their rage.

My own child died in a world of random error. To whom can
I hurl my anger when the only villains are an oak tree, a vine, a
hand that slipped, an arm that could not reach out fast enough to
stop a fall? What I need is a target for my rage that is the size of
a madman, a serial killer.

"Uh-huh," I hear Harold saying as I close my journal. "This
one today be number nineteen, and that boy you be telling me
about, the one what died a year ago this week, be number twelve.
It break your heart, don't it, Miz Margaret?"

"Number eleven," I say, correcting him. Harold's tentative,
apologetic tone has begun to annoy me. "His name was Carl."

"Yes, ma'am."

"He was only nine years old, but a mother can't protect her
children every minute of the day."

"That's the truth! Uh-huh."

"She can worry, of course. She can wait for a neighbor to ring her doorbell to let her know her little boy forgot to look both ways before he crossed the street. Or her daughter forgot the swimming pool was too shallow for diving. Or the hunter forgot to notice that her son's camouflage shirt wasn't a deer."

Harold rubs his ear and then runs his hand over the jagged scar that follows the line of his jaw. "Lord Jesus."

"Or somebody gets drunk. Your daughter's date, or your son, or the other driver. And you lie awake in bed and watch the clock, Harold. There's a siren somewhere screaming through the night, and you wait for the telephone call you've dreaded all their lives. And while you wait, you can even see the car in your mind's eye. You can see it lying upside down on some lonely street or other, the wheels spinning and the headlights aimed through the upper branches of a tree . . ."

I stop. Harold and Earllovette have no children. How in the hell could he even begin to understand?

"I knows what you mean, Miz Margaret. Been worried many a time about Jimmy since Mr. Bridges done give him that fancy car."

"But you can never imagine the *real* ending," I say, turning away from him to look off into the distance at the skyline of the city. "One minute you're in your den watching a movie on television and the next minute you're the mother of a dead child."

"Meg be her own self, Miz Margaret. If she want to go back to them woods and climb a tree like she done when she was a little girl, ain't nobody on earth could of stopped her."

"Did I worry about the woods when they were young?"

"Yes, ma'am."

"I don't remember. I stopped thinking about those woods a long time ago. They were just some place I used to play when I was a child. Too swampy for anybody to build houses on, I thought. And now Mr. Matthews has leveled the land all the way to the train trestle, brought in mounds of topsoil, and it's another exclusive subdivision coming, Harold. Nobody will ever know where my daughter died. It will just be somebody's basement."

"Uh-huh. Meg sure enough be her own self. Didn't take nothing off nobody, did she?"

We sit in silence for a moment, thinking our own thoughts. Then I hear Harold chuckling to himself.

"What?"

"Be remembering that time Meg done come out to the backyard to find me, she be about six or seven, sassy as a jaybird, and she asks me straight out why some black folks smell funny. 'Meg Bridges,' I say, 'your mama going to get you good. Black folks don't smell no funnier than white folks. We be all equal in our smells.'" Harold shakes his head and laughs. "But she be right, Miz Margaret. Smart as a judge, that child. She took me by the hand and led me into the kitchen and make me take a whiff of that high-yellow maid what worked for us a couple of months one time. Remember? Corrina was her name, I think. She done been stealing your vanilla to put behind her ears. Smelled like boiled custard. Uh-huh. Smelled *real* funny, Miz Margaret. No! Don't nobody ever put nothing over on *that* little girl. Meg sure enough could tell it like it was."

"It's getting late, Harold," I say. "Go on across the street and borrow taxi fare from Jimmy. Earllovette's probably got supper waiting for you, and you must be hungry."

"No, ma'am. Had plenty to eat while you ladies was having your garden meeting. And Meg say: 'Harold, you going to miss me when I go off to college?' And I say: 'Huh. The one be going to miss somebody be *you*.' Uh-huh. Last thing I ever say to her. Tell that girl she going to miss me. And look what she gone and done."

I look up from my lap.

"It be *me* what's had to do the missing."

I don't answer. I watch Harold shaking his head, twisting the gloves in his lap. But when I see the tears welled up in his eyes, I turn away and quickly open my journal.

"I been meaning all this time to tell you something, Miz Margaret."

Don't.

"Earllovette and me feel real bad we wasn't with you all that day. Uh-huh. We was at home. Planting tomatoes."

I can't think of anything to say. I hardly know Harold's wife. It's never occurred to me that Harold wasn't around when Meg died. He wasn't supposed to be, it was a Saturday. I don't even know how he found out about it, and until this moment I've never thought to ask.

"We was out in the garden when Miz Matthews called. Planting butter beans."

Butter beans, I write in large spidery letters across the bottom of the page. *Tomatoes. And I was cleaning up the house. It was the morning after the garden club party and I had to empty the ashtrays. Unload the dishwasher. Put away the silver. I had to pack the leftover bazaar items in boxes, fold the card tables, hide them in the Secret Room under the staircase. I had to make up the beds. Pick Meg and Jimmy's clothes off the floor and hang them in their closets. Eleven o'clock. I had to call Ida. I had to call my mother back. I had to fix lunch.*

"Lunch," I read out loud, hearing the word, finding the sound of it strange.

And while I waited for Peter to get back home from his golf game, I poured myself a cup of coffee and lay down on the den sofa.

"That's the worst part, Harold. That's the part I can't stop thinking about. Because all the time Jimmy was sawing the vine with his pocketknife and all the time he was showing Meg where to grab hold of it—the moment she let herself go—I was watching a movie on television. When she died, I was somewhere else. I keep hearing the vine snap, Harold. I keep hearing the surprise in her voice when she starts falling. But I can't push it beyond that, Harold. She never lands on the ground. The ending has no sound."

I cover my ears. I close my eyes to click off the television set in the den. But the picture is always there. I am leaning forward on the sofa, taking a sip of coffee . . .

10

The *Newswatch* camera was scanning the scene being described by the professionally dispassionate reporter: the steep embankment, the tangled underbrush, the kudzu-shrouded trees looming in the background like beasts from a child's nightmare. As the camera panned away from the dwarfed figure of a young police officer crouching beside a green plastic body bag and panned back up the embankment to capture the faces of those standing in isolated groups behind the police barricades, the voice of the reporter broke under the stress of the witnesses' twisted smiles of pain and embarrassment, their eager eyes of curiosity, their blank stares of shock and horror.

"According to the sanitation . . . worker who discovered the . . . child . . . shortly after arriving for work this . . . morning, the body appears to be that of a black male, perhaps nine or ten years . . ."

"Thank you for that report," a voice cut in. "If the body is indeed one of the missing children, it will bring the official murder count to eleven . . ."

I went into the kitchen. Poured another cup of coffee. Returned to the den.

"And now we return to our regular programming. Tune in for more details on *Afternoon News* at three o'clock . . ."

Cary Grant leaned against a railing at the top of the Empire State Building. Deborah Kerr lay in a hospital bed, miles away.

"Where's Meg?" Peter asked from the doorway. He removed his jogging cap. He combed his fingers through his thin hair. "What's Jimmy doing?"

"They're off somewhere."

He walked over to the sofa, leaned down and kissed me on the back of the neck. "You and that movie," he said, glancing up in time to see Cary turn away from the view of New York City in a thunderstorm and move disconsolately toward the elevator doors. "I'd think you and Meg would be sick to death of it by now."

"Yes."

Deborah's priest took her hand. "Won't you let us tell him the truth?"

"I'm going to take a shower, Margaret. And then I'm going to play a round of golf at the club."

"Uh-huh."

Cary hunched his shoulders against the rain.

"No," Deborah said, smiling bravely. "Not until I can learn to run to him again . . ."

———

"Times have changed," Meg told me that morning when I went into her bedroom to wake her up. We'd all slept late because of the party the night before.

"You've got it all wrong," I said. "I wasn't talking about you, darling. I was talking about other kinds of girls."

She didn't answer. She was furious with me. Embarrassed perhaps. Maybe scared.

"What on earth can you know about love at your age?"

"Ha!" Jimmy said, smirking.

"Where does she think she's going?" I asked him. "You go after your sister and tell her to come back here immediately."

"Aw, Mom."

"And don't argue with me. I will not have her running out on her mother when I still have plenty more to say."

———

Three o'clock. Do you know where your children are?

I was unloading the dishwasher.

I was gathering the dirty napkins from the party and carrying them down to the laundry room in the basement.

I was upstairs in Meg's room, taking the new dress she was going to wear to graduation out of the closet.

I was back on the den sofa, opening my sewing basket, clicking on the television, watching the news.

"The body discovered earlier today behind an office complex on Carver Drive has been identified as Carl Taylor, missing for fourteen weeks."

I went into the kitchen.

Where in the world were Jimmy and Meg? They'd been gone for hours. They couldn't possibly still be in the woods. It was absolutely typical of them not to tell me they were going off somewhere.

I looked in the garage. Meg's car was there. They had probably gone to the park, or to one of the neighbors' houses.

I returned to the kitchen. Made a few telephone calls. To Jimmy's friend, Arnold Matthews. To Meg's friend, Lucie Earle Johnson. To Bobby Turner.

"Have you seen Meg? Is Jimmy over there?"

I called Daddy. I called Ida. I called Mary Earle. I walked next door to see Mrs. Dahlbender. Where in the hell was Peter? Why wasn't he back from golf?

"Jimmy!" I was calling through the woods. "Meg!"

Four o'clock. Do you know . . .?

"She fell," Jimmy said, when I finally found them. "It was an accident," he kept saying after the police ambulance drove her away and after we came home from the funeral and after my friends came to sit with me in the living room for days and weeks to talk about *whys* and *if onlys*. "I would have saved her if I could," he kept saying over and over again. "Don't talk about it, darling," I answered. I couldn't bear the thought of Jimmy kneeling so long in the woods beside his sister's body. "Let's just remember how special Meg was when she was alive."

Yes. I was terrified that if he talked too much about her death, I'd forget her life. Everything that had been my daughter would disappear into nothing except that one moment at the end when her head hit the ground.

"Shhh," I said. "Shhh."

And so we talked of other things:

"The call of the brown thrasher," Peter said at the breakfast table the morning he returned from an Audubon field trip on the property Arnold Matthews was buying to develop into Atlanta's most exclusive new suburban subdivision, "is a simple *smack*!"

"The veins of a dogwood leaf," I said at the dinner table one evening after Harold and I had planted three small trees in our new red-clay yard, "curve upwards toward a smooth and wavy margin."

"The combination of a negative and a positive in a single print," Jimmy explained in the darkroom the night his father left us, "is called the Sabattier effect."

"Yet another grim discovery," a voice on Annie D.'s television set said this morning as I marched out the door on my way to the garden club meeting. "It brings the total number of murdered Atlanta children to eighteen."

———

"Stop talking about it, Margaret," Joyce Belinda ordered. She leaned forward in her lawn chair. "I'm sick and tired of hearing about dead colored children."

Yes. And Cynthia Foster and Patsy Pierson were sick of dead children. And Ida and Georgina Watkins and Bootsey Kelley and all the other members of the garden club were tired of hearing black celebrities in town stirring up blame and suspicion. Weary unto death of black mothers stirring up guilt and fear.

"If you ask me," Mirabelle Harris said, "there *is* no madman on the loose in Atlanta. This so-called list of missing and murdered children is just another example of nigra paranoia." She removed a plastic wine glass from the tray Harold was passing and lowered her voice. "It's simply a fabrication invented by all those b-l-a-c-k people who have taken over City Hall."

Bootsey Kelley narrowed her eyes knowingly at Mirabelle. "I wouldn't be at all surprised if they find out that it's the children's fathers behind all these killings."

"Their fathers?" Joyce Belinda shook her head in disbelief. "Those little boys don't *have* fathers, Bootsey. And their mothers let them run around by themselves on the streets at all hours of the day and night." She glared over at me. "I can assure you I'd never allow *my* child to run around by herself at all hours of the day and night."

"A mother can't always know where her children are," Ida said quickly, not looking at me. "Sometimes the best a mother can do is worry."

Cynthia was tugging on the sleeve of my pioneer blouse. "*Margaret!* What if all those outsiders writing ugly things about us turn out to be right? What if it really *is* the Ku Klux Klan killing black children? We'd have riots! We'd never be able to leave our houses, we'd be prisoners in our own *homes*."

"For goodness sakes, Cynthia, close your mouth," Georgina said. "You're blowing this whole thing out of proportion. Anyway, they're not killing children in Buckhead."

No. And they were not killing children in Arcadia Heights. We were miles from the killings. While the girls discussed the morning news and the morning paper, I forced my mind to click away from the image of a child's body being placed inside a green plastic bag. I concentrated instead on Ida's backyard. The beds of tulips and daffodils filled the edges of her patio with a slightly mildewy odor. The towhee on her crabapple tree was making a noise that sounded something like *drink-your-TEA, drink-your-TEA* . . .

"Lunch, Miz Margaret?"

I could tell by Harold's voice that he was embarrassed. A white butler's jacket covered his shirt, and the little wicker picnic basket he was holding out to me in his huge hand was tied up in feminine ribbons of blue and yellow. I recognized one of the silver forks Ida had borrowed from me the day before.

"What can you do with tacky people like that?" I heard Georgina asking.

"Do with whom?" I asked. I'd missed something. Apparently the girls were no longer discussing the latest murder victim.

"They move to Atlanta," Joyce Belinda said, ignoring me, "and think if they buy a house on West Paces Ferry Road they're automatically guaranteed a membership in the Carriage Country Club."

"Isn't that the truth?" Patsy Pierson cried. "And they come down here and try to change everything. If they don't like the way we live in the South, they ought to stay where they are."

"New rich . . ."

"Tearing down every old building in sight . . ."

"Money, money, money . . ."

I stopped listening to the stories about outsiders coming to Atlanta and started listening to other noises. Somewhere in the neighborhood, dogs were barking. Buzz saws were taking down one of Mrs. Ferguson's beetle-rotted pine trees. Trucks driving along the access road of U.S. 41 kept shifting gears going up the steep incline on the other side of Ida's ten-foot-high boxwood hedge. Every once in a while one of the garden club ladies would have to stop talking in mid-sentence to wait for the end to yet another series of horns honking down at the intersection of Hercules and Demeter.

"What on earth is that racket?" Cynthia finally asked.

"It's just the high school kids celebrating spring break," Ida explained at the top of her lungs. "They're going to drive me crazy. I told Little Arnold to stay the hell out of the house today so we could have some peace and quiet for the meeting, and what does he do? He calls up all his friends to go rafting down the Chattahoochee this afternoon, and now half his class is hanging around here before they leave."

Jimmy knew about the rafting trip, Ida had invited him when

she called the house this morning, but I had no idea whether or not he'd decided to join Little Arnold's friends. My son never confided his plans to his mother any longer. Instead, he took pictures of her and spread them across the kitchen counter so they'd be the last thing she'd see as she walked out the door: a woman in a blue cocktail dress lying flopped across the sofa. A woman with legs spread apart, with a mouth hanging open in a drunken gape.

"We love living only a mile from the river," I heard Ida shouting as I mentally ripped the photographs to shreds and tossed them into the trashmasher. "But what Arnold and I love best about Arcadia Heights is that we have all the security of the suburbs, yet we're practically living in the very bosom of downtown Atlanta! Why, the other day our yardman, Harold, was up on the roof repairing our weather vane, and he called down to me that he could actually see the skyline of the city. Imagine! He said it looked like . . ."

A diesel truck suddenly shifted gears going up the access road on the other side of Ida's boxwood hedge. I missed the end of her sentence.

"After a while," Ida continued, as the grind of the truck was replaced by the roar of a police siren racing down U.S. 41, "the sound of traffic becomes just as natural as a waterfall. It becomes a sound you don't even hear!"

"Like the music they play at the A&P!" Mirabelle sang out. She pointed a knitting needle in the direction of the hedge.

I wasn't so sure. The high school kids were making noises at the intersection that I found difficult to ignore. It wasn't just the horns honking, but their loud laughter, their voices hollering out to one another, their car radios turned to different music stations so it became impossible to unravel one tune from another.

I pictured their jeeps and station wagons and vans clogging the streets. Mothers bringing their children home from ballet classes and horseback riding lessons and T-ball games would be forced to come to a stop before easing around the groups of teenagers standing so arrogantly in the middle of the road.

I tried to visualize Jimmy the way he would have been a year ago, down at the corner with the others. Cut-off jeans. T-shirt. Dirty sneakers. Loading his raft and ice cooler into the back of Little Arnold's van, or sitting on the hood of my station wagon while a girl flirted with him, her hand touching his arm, her smile trained on the dark hair that used to curl at the back of his neck.

Another series of honking horns: *Dah-dah-de-dah-dah.*

I closed my eyes and placed Jimmy and the girl inside his new Spitfire convertible. She leaned across him to reach the steering wheel. With the palm of her hand, she beat out the answer to their friend's greeting. *Dah. Dah.*

"I can assure you I'd never allow a child of *mine* to honk a horn like that," I imagined Joyce Belinda announcing. "If Lucie Earle even so much as *thought* about honking a horn like that . . ."

"*Margaret,*" Cynthia wailed, interrupting my thoughts. "Did you hear about that poor mother last week who accidentally placed her baby—he was in an infant seat—on top of her car while she looked through her pocketbook for the car keys? And she drove six miles down the expressway before she remembered where she'd left him?"

"That's nothing," Bootsey said. "I was at my hair dresser's the other day and this woman told me about a mother on Peachtree Battle Avenue—I can't remember her name, but you all would know her—who allowed her nine-year-old daughter to stick her head out of the back window, and it got knocked completely off by a telephone pole."

"Oh, that happens all the time," Patsy said. "But if you really want to hear something terrible, did you all read about that little three-year-old boy from southwest Atlanta who put the cat instead of the milk bottle in the refrigerator all night last week?"

"Oh, well," somebody said. "Southwest Atlanta. What can you expect?"

"And did you hear . . .?" asked Cynthia. "And did you hear . . .?" asked a lady named Claudia somebody, who was only at the meeting because she was visiting Mirabelle from some little town in Alabama nobody knew what to call.

"And did you hear . . .?"

The horrors of daily life, whether in downtown Atlanta or in the suburbs, began circling the lawn chairs of Ida's backyard. The mother who had allowed her teenage daughter to flush her brother's guppies down the toilet, and naturally they'd immediately begun to *breed*. So now, although the mayor would have you believe this was merely an urban myth being perpetuated by white people angry at all the blacks in City Hall, the water system in Atlanta was absolutely *filthy* with guppy poo-poo. The mother who had allowed her teenage son to buy that new candy that was *supposed*, they'd said, to only *feel* like it was exploding inside your mouth . . .

While the stories gained momentum, I heard somebody near me exclaim loudly over the noise of the buzz saws: "You can't imagine what it's like to have a father-in-law who calls you every single morning to read you the obituary column, who wakes you up every single day of your entire life to give you the history of every person who has died since the night before. Can you imagine what that's like?"

I was trying to, when Harold leaned over to take away my lunch basket. He sneered down at my partially nibbled frozen fruit salad, at the bite taken from the slice of Honey Baked ham. "Uh-huh. Ain't done even a canary's worth," he said.

"Girls?" Bootsey shouted, calling the April meeting of the Buckhead Garden Club to order from in front of the birdbath, which Ida had changed into a podium by draping a blue and yellow checkered tablecloth over it to match the ribbons on the lunch baskets. "Shall we pray?"

To the sounds of the towhees and buzz saws and the barking dogs and the car radios, we bowed our heads and recited the official club prayer: "Prune, weed and fertilize our souls, O Lord. Grant that we may grow ever more beautiful in Thy sight."

As soon as the last "amen" was uttered, Bootsey called me to the podium to read from the minutes of the March meeting:

Officer Richard Garcia of the Buckhead Precinct presented an informative program entitled "How to Protect Yourself Against Muggers and Rapists."
1. When walking down the sidewalk, remember who you are and where you're going. Stride confidently.
2. Keep your car keys clutched firmly between your knuckles at all times, to be used, if absolutely necessary, as a defensive weapon.
3. Be assertive. Look your potential assailant straight in the eye.
4. Nobody cares pee-squat about anybody but himself these days. Therefore, when attacked, don't waste your breath screaming *Help!* Instead, yell *Fire!* and immediately kick directly at the assailant's You Know Whats.

Cynthia followed me to the podium with her civic project report on *A Child's Alphabet Guide to Atlanta*, the book we'd recently completed writing for distribution to underprivileged kindergartners.

"A is for Antebellum homes . . ." Cynthia began.

"Reproductions," Georgina whispered.

"B is for Beautiful parks . . ."

"Taken over by the queers."

"C is for Christian churches . . ."

I glanced around at the ladies of the garden club. We'd been together for over fifteen years, but some of them I'd known since childhood. It occurred to me we'd written the alphabet book too late. We should have written it the year of our founding, the year we were all wearing miniskirts and Jackie Kennedy wigs and taking courses in Parent Effectiveness Training. Today we were all dressed in calf-length skirts and designer boots. Most of us didn't know any children who were learning their ABC's. The children we knew had already learned how to fake their I.D.'s.

I stopped listening after "D is for Dogwoods, blossoming in spring . . ." Instead, I began making a mental list of all the classes and projects we'd done together as a club over the years. A kind of alphabet guide to women in their forties: Aerobic dancing . . . Bread-dough ornaments . . . Collecting Chinese porcelains . . . Duplicate bridge . . .

I thought of my mother. Although she was very weak for a long time after she returned from the tuberculosis hospital, she still managed to be interested in all kinds of classes and projects. Her dream, she told me years later, had been to make a pile of money so she could pay Daddy back for every red cent he'd ever spent on keeping Grandmother Leticia out of the poorhouse.

When I was quite young, Mother would lie on her chaise lounge and knit baby booties. "I'm developing a pattern," she'd explain whenever Beatrice took me into the bedroom to visit her. "And after I've gotten the pattern right, I'll hire your father's bakery ladies to knit up the booties in their spare time. We'll form a cooperative. We'll sell booties all over the country. We'll have a business together just as nice as your father's business. Do you understand, dear?"

Yes. I understood. And after Mother became well enough to spend most of her day off the chaise lounge, she discovered china painting. Ida's mother and Joyce Belinda and Mary Earle's mother would meet in our den and work all afternoon at card tables set up with little brushes and bottles of gold paint. "We're developing an assembly line," Ida's mother explained. "Each of us will specialize on different letters of the alphabet. We'll soon be monogramming these dishes so fast, your head will spin. We'll be accepting orders from all over the world!"

They had been happy, those women. But after a while they stopped gilding china cups and saucers and dinner plates in our den, and Mother started entering contests. The desk in her bed-room would be covered with scraps of notebook paper. Even more scraps would be wadded up and tossed on the floor. I would come home from school and find her groaning to herself as she searched desperately through her Thesaurus and rhyming dictionary for ways to write something clever about Vitalis or Borateam or Duz.

When somebody with the Maxwell House Coffee Company came out with "Leaves No Grounds for Complaint," Mother became distraught. "That was exactly what *I* was going to write!" she said. "Somebody went and stole that idea right out of my head, Margaret! Can you believe that?"

Yes. I could believe that.

"Darn it!" my mother said. "It isn't as easy as you might think, dear."

No. And when the Burma-Shave people rejected all of Mother's ideas for road signs, she decided to give up contests. She switched to making shell earrings with Mrs. Dahlbender. All afternoon the two of them would sit at our breakfast table, dipping tiny pastel-tinted seashells into glue.

"I've never been able to express myself clearly," Mother said sadly when I asked her why she had stopped writing. "I've never had anything to say that would be of interest."

Poor Mother! She never had the opportunity her daughter would have one day to hear a famous Atlanta authoress speak on the subject of creative writing: "All it takes to write is to know what you want to say, and then just say it!"

"But aren't there certain rules you have to follow?" somebody asked.

"The first rule," Babs explained, "is to choose the proper point of view. Who is telling the story?"

Ah, we had that. The Buckhead Garden Club was telling the story. Each of us had drawn a Scrabble tile from Mary Earle's sterling silver calling card tray. Every member of the club had her own personal assignment. My assignment was "Z."

"The second rule of good writing," my sister-in-law continued, "is to establish genre. Is this to be a mystery? A romance? A science fiction story?"

We had that, too. *A Child's Alphabet Guide to Atlanta* was to be an instructional, a tool to teach little public school children their letters.

"And finally," she continued, "you have to begin at the beginning."

Yes! Bootsey Kelley had drawn the letter "A."

"Then it just becomes a matter of expanding that," Babs explained. "You add a middle and an end."

The middle had been easy.

"M is for MARTA buses . . ." Cynthia was reading aloud to us at the top of her lungs. "N is for Neiman-Marcus . . . O is for Oil paintings at the High Museum of Art . . ."

But I had suffered agonies trying to come up with a good ending. "What begins with 'Z'?" I'd asked Jimmy.

"Zoom lenses," he'd answered, looking up from a photograph he was examining through a loupe. "Zinc sulfate."

"No, darling. Something fun for little children."

"Zen Buddhism, Zoroastrianism, Zionism," Meg suggested.

I called my mother.

"Zebra?" she asked doubtfully. "Zinnia?"

"Dammit to hell!" I raged the night Peter came into the den of our old house in Buckhead and found me surrounded by piles of wadded-up notebook paper. "Can you believe this? It's impossible! I'll never be able to come up with a good ending if it takes the rest of my life!"

"Zoo," he said. "Did you remember to take my shirts to the laundry?"

"I want something original, Peter."

"Come on, Margaret. I *need* those shirts! You didn't forget, did you?"

"Yes. Here's what I want, Peter. I want something that the children will know about already, but because of me, they'll begin to think about it in a new and exciting way."

"Jesus! You mean you didn't go to the laundry because of this one letter of the alphabet? Just write anything. Put down *Zeus*. It won't make any difference."

But he was wrong. It *did* make a difference.

"Z is for jet planes at the Atlanta Airport," Cynthia was reading, finally at the end of the book.

I felt the eyes of the garden club staring at me. I felt their mouths drop open.

"Z is for jet planes?" Cynthia asked. "Is that what you meant to write, Margaret?"

I caught Harold by his white butler's jacket. I grabbed another drink.

"Zany, Zestful *Zooms?*" Cynthia asked.

———

Oh, I've always loved the members of the Buckhead Garden Club! They can laugh longer and harder than any other people I know. And even though they sometimes ridicule you, embarrass you, talk for hours about you behind your back, they will forgive you anything at all. And when they are through laughing at a certain girl who has an extremely difficult time coming up with good endings, and when they are through laughing over their stories about mothers who allow their children to contaminate the sewer with guppy poo and have finished their sighings over the brains of a little boy who can't tell the difference between a cat and a milk bottle, they can settle back quietly in their lawn chairs and listen attentively to Joyce Belinda announce the next year's civic project.

But to tell the truth, when Joyce Belinda began showing us Mary Earle's draft dodgers that hadn't sold at last year's bazaar— "gaily colored tubes of cotton filled with twenty pounds of sand" —and when she began explaining just how many more we'd have to make in order to serve all the underprivileged mothers who lived in poorly insulated public housing units and needed something to put on their windowsills to ward off the chills of winter, I started having serious doubts about the intelligence of some of the members of the garden club. Our draft dodgers were going to be delivered, Joyce Belinda said, to welfare recipients in the heart of downtown Atlanta.

"Are you insane?" Patsy asked the minute Bootsey opened the proposal for discussion. "I wouldn't be caught dead going downtown. Nobody goes downtown these days!"

"And why should we?" Georgina wanted to know. She stopped poking thread in and out of the needlepoint golf club cover she was making for the next bazaar long enough to add: "We have far more desirable shopping right in our own neighborhoods."

"And more desirable people!" Bootsey shouted.

"*Margaret,*" Cynthia said, clutching at my pioneer skirt, "will you promise to go with me? I'd be afraid to try to kick a rapist in his You Know Whats."

Yes. And the ladies of the garden club would be afraid of purse snatchers. Oglers. Graffiti on the sidewalk. What if they accidentally stepped in spit?

"Besides," Patsy said, "what would we ever find to do downtown if we went? Who on earth would even know who we were?"

"Shut up," Joyce Belinda yelled. "You're all behaving like a bunch of idiots. Did I say one word about your having to go downtown? Did I say anything whatsoever to lead you to think I was expecting you to deliver the draft dodgers yourselves? I most certainly did not." She looked at me sharply. "I discussed this with Mary Earle last night *at length,* and I'm helping her arrange to have the dodgers delivered by UPS."

Oh.

The ladies settled back once again in their lawn chairs. They smiled and let their eyes wander over Ida's lovely yard. A beautiful spring day out in the suburbs. Yes. And Ida was right, after all. The sounds in the background were almost exactly like a waterfall. One hardly noticed the flow of buzz saws and diesel engines and birds, the teenagers and their radios.

To the murmurs of conversations about children and husbands and tubes of cotton filled with sand, I started thinking about Jimmy again, imagining him with Little Arnold's crowd down at the intersection. *It's not too late for you to be popular again.* I took off his army surplus uniform and dressed him in his old pair of sawed-off jeans. *Wear what the others wear.* I placed him in the middle of the street with his hands shoved inside his front pockets—just the thumbs showing—and I made him nod agree-ably to the driver of the car turning the corner. *Carnegie's Rules in a Nutshell, darling: Smile. Make the other fellow feel important.*

But something was wrong with Jimmy's smile. Something was . . . Wait! Something was happening with the car that wasn't supposed to happen. I held my breath against the long wailing *screech!* of the tires. I half rose in my chair and reached my arms out to push my son away from the dull *thud*, the sounds of glass shattering, people shouting.

I looked around me in horror. My friends had already aban-doned their lawn chairs. "Harold! Call an ambulance!" Joyce Belinda was shouting as she ran with the others across the drive-way toward the embankment on the other side of the boxwood hedge.

"No!" Ida yelled, stopping them. "You won't be able to get past the cyclone fence down there! Come with me!"

Immediately, in a reflex response to years of Red Cross train-ing, lifesaving classes, lessons in CPR, my friends turned as one to hurry down the driveway after her.

I didn't move.

Where was Jimmy?

"Splints!" Cynthia shouted, rushing out of the house with Ida's tennis racket. She snatched the tablecloth from the birdbath as she ran past it. "Bandages!"

I turned my head in the direction of the intersection. Some-one's scream was rising above the other noises. "He's dead!" an old woman was screaming. "You've killed him!"

Three o'clock. Do you know where your children are?

———

A mother can imagine all sorts of terrible endings when she is sitting in a lawn chair wrapping a fog around her shoulders like a shawl. And every ending she imagines, she prays to change. *Don't do this to Peter and me again, God. Don't let it be our Jimmy.*

She would not discover the *true* terrible ending until she had risen from her chair and, protected by prayer and fog, walked across a driveway and pushed her way through a six-foot-high boxwood hedge. Half stumbling, half sliding down an embankment, she was not even aware of her boots catching in the underbrush, of her hands tearing through the tangles of briars and vines. She was aware only of a dreadful need to reach the cyclone fence, to strain to see through the thick stand of kudzu-shrouded pine trees and dogwoods on the other side.

Whether she was fifty feet from the intersection, or only twenty, does not matter. Even the sight of a twisted car near the curb was unessential to her purpose: to make sense of the rest of the scene. The movements of shirts and dresses, the confusion of excited voices, the screams of an old woman wailing, "You've killed him!"

Jimmy.

She edged along the fence in a crouch.

"Murderer!"

"No! It was just an accident, lady!"

Ah, Jimmy. At the sound of her son's denial, she sank to her knees in gratitude. *You're alive. Thank you, God.*

But why was she now digging her fingernails into her bare arms? *It was just an accident.* Why, as other voices rose to her son's defense in garbled, incoherent protests—"No!" . . . "It was" . . . "meant to hurt" . . . "accident!" . . . "your husband, lady!"—did she feel the chill of exposure prickling the skin at the back of her neck? *No crime has been committed here . . .*

"Dear God," she heard herself groaning over and over again as she stared at her hand gripping the cyclone fence, at the streak of blood near the thumb where a briar had torn it. If she stared at her hand long enough, she wouldn't have to hear the sirens screaming down U.S. 41. *Why hadn't he run home and told her Meg was hurt?* She wouldn't have to think about the ladies of the Buckhead Garden Club now crowding around the body that lay wedged between two trees on the other side of the fence. *Why had he hidden from her all those hours in the woods?*

Yes. If she refused to take her eyes off the thin streak of blood

11

The ladies of the Buckhead Garden Club. The woman kneeling by the cyclone fence had known them all for more than fifteen years. Some, like Ida and Joyce Belinda and Mary Earle and Cynthia and Georgina, she'd known since childhood. "Sandbox friends," they called themselves.

When they were young, when time was measured not by clocks or public service announcements on television but by voices rising in a hallway or calling from a backdoor stoop ("I'm going to be late for work! Where did you hide my briefcase, Charlotte?" . . . "Put away your flexi racers, children, and come to supper!"), they were heroines.

While their parents whispered behind their backs about the poor little boy from Oklahoma who had fallen down a well, they lowered themselves on ropes and pulled him to safety. When the police kept grilling the artist from Buckhead whose wife was found strangled to death near a creek behind a house on Howell Mill Road, they studied the clues in their scrapbooks of newspaper clippings and identified the real killer as a member of a chain gang that had been working on the Howell Mill Road bridge the day of the murder.

They married Prince Phillip, testified on television before the McCarthy hearings, rescued the Rosenbergs from the electric chair, climbed Mount Everest, invented a polio vaccine, took actual photographs of a flying saucer from Mars.

When they got older, they were going to be mannequins in a window at Rich's department store—*"Aren't they pretty?"* one of their grandmothers asked the week before she climbed to the roof of the downtown library and jumped. And when they were grown, they were going to become nurses and teachers and missionaries. They were going to find a cure for cancer, win the Cold War, wipe out world hunger.

But something happened. Ida Matthews was the only one among them who grew up to be pretty. And none of them grew up to be great. Instead, they became the ladies who lunch. The ladies who give charity balls. The ladies who lead school groups through the High Museum of Art, or sell old clothes at the Nearly New Shop, or stuff envelopes at the Atlanta Historical Society.

If, along the way, a few of them read *The Feminine Mystique* and changed their minds, they discovered they had already gone too far to change their lives.

"Liberation?" they asked themselves. Liberation from what? Liberation *for* what? That was for younger women, poor women, minority women, single women. The best one of them could do was try to pass the improbable dream along to her daughter. ("Stop complaining, Meg. If you don't like the way things are, then work to correct them; don't just sit there pouting. You don't have any idea how it used to be when I was your age. You don't know *beans* about how much has been done for you by these women your grandfather calls 'libbers.' Look at you! You can do anything you want to with your life.")

And if, at times, some of the members of the Buckhead Garden Club found themselves waking up in the middle of the night alarmed over having dreamed they had become irrelevant; if, at times, they walked by a mirror in a hallway or took a sip of coffee in a neighbor's kitchen and suddenly saw themselves as they knew others must see them—trivial rich ladies leading trivial rich lives—they could take consolation in the fact that it would have taken a miracle for any of them to have ended up differently. And at their age, did anyone believe in miracles anymore?

No. The ladies of the garden club knew how to advise their husbands on what to wear to work and keep them company on their important business conventions. They knew how to drive car pools and cheer for their children in school plays and sports competitions. They knew how to give lovely dinner parties, listen to each other's problems, laugh at each other's jokes. And the self-deprecating humor they used to charm the world came easily to them. It had been honed since birth.

So what did it really matter that they weren't heroines? They hadn't grown up to be great, that's true, but they had all managed to grow up to be very, very good. They were moral people. Yes. They were the kind of people who could be depended upon to do what was expected, to do what was right.

When the security and propriety of their world was threatened by the sounds of screeching tires and the thud of metal, they took immediate action. And when they realized that none of their classes in lifesaving and none of their lessons in CPR could bring back a dead man, they knew how to do the common, decent things: They consoled his widow.

They waited with her on the sidewalk until the ambulance had come and gone, until the wrecker had disappeared, until someone had driven her back to her house and all the other onlookers had been sent on their way to raft down the Chattahoochee River. And then, reluctantly and sadly, they returned up the Matthews's driveway to resume their meeting in the finest backyard in Arcadia Heights.

"Our Father, Who art in heaven," they prayed, "comfort those in grief and show the paths of righteousness to those who have lost their way."

And after they had paid their respects to the old man who died, after they had paused to acknowledge their common endings, the ladies of the Buckhead Garden Club settled back in their lawn chairs and listened to one of their members finish her story about a cousin whose college roommate grew up next door to a boy from Memphis who had actually known the brother of the girl who had died when hornets nested in her beehive hairdo and stung her to death.

And after Cynthia's tale was over, and after somebody remembered the name of a friend who had the same manicurist as the mother who had allowed her child to flush live guppies down the toilet, it was time to return to the official business of adopting a civic project. Joyce Belinda Johnson rose to propose her sister's draft dodgers. Mirabelle Harris seconded. Bootsey Kelley called for discussion. Or so the woman kneeling by the cyclone fence imagined.

While the members of the club were debating the merits of sand and cotton, she was still trying to wrap herself in a fog. Her face was still buried in her hands.

"Mom?"

She didn't look up at the sound of her son coming down the embankment.

"What are you doing here, Mom?" he asked, crouching beside her. "Did you see the accident?"

She shook her head.

"It was crazy! Everybody was just standing around in the street, minding their own business, when this car came around the corner. It made a big deal of slowing down almost to a crawl, and when it finally went past, Billy Ferguson reached out and banged his hand on the trunk. The driver went wild! He was this real old guy, Mom, and he slammed his foot on the accelerator instead of the brake, and he jerked the steering wheel straight toward the Matthews's telephone pole."

She raised her head, without looking at him. "Billy Ferguson," she said coldly.

"Poor bastard," Jimmy said.

"Billy Ferguson?" she repeated, wheeling around on her knees. "*He's* the one who killed that poor woman's husband?"

"No, Mom. I told you. It was the old guy's own fault. He should have . . ."

She heard the hesitation, the low groan. She looked over to where her son was staring.

"Christ," he groaned.

"Don't look," she said, staring herself at the old man's shoe propped against the other side of the fence, half buried in the underbrush.

She heard him scrambling to his feet, turned to see his face contorted in horror, curiosity, pain.

"It's all right," she said.

He was still looking at the shoe.

She reached up to wrap her arms around his knees. "It wasn't your fault," she said.

He pushed her away. "Leave me alone."

"No. I should never have sent you after her. I should have gone after her myself."

"Goddamnit," he moaned, suddenly doubling over to hug himself.

"Ah, Jimmy. Listen to me. It's—"

"God*damn* it!" he howled, jerking backwards. "I hate that old guy for dying!" He turned toward the embankment, sobbing with fury.

"No!" She grabbed the back of his camouflage trousers, tugged on them. "If you want to hate somebody, hate *me*." She sank down miserably at his feet.

"Don't, Mom." He wiped at his eyes with his fists. "Get up before somebody sees you."

"It was all my fault!" she cried, looking up at him pleadingly.

"Jesus." He'd stopped crying. He was glaring down at her with his father's expression of self-control. Condescension. Disgust. "Lower your voice," he whispered. "Everybody's already back up on Mrs. Matthews's patio. They'll hear you."

"They'll *hear* me?" She pulled herself to her feet. "A man is dead because of you kids, and that's all you're worried about?"

"Come on, Mom."

"I thought you were *dead*! Do you realize that? When I heard the sound of tires skidding, I thought they were skidding straight at *you*!"

"Shhhh."

She lunged for him and tried to reach his chest with her fists. "Then I thought it was *you* in that car! I thought it was *you* screeching down the street in that stupid convertible your father gave you. Yes! I thought it was *you* who killed that old man!"

"Calm down," he whispered. He gripped her wrists and held her away from him. "You always think the worst. Stop acting hysterical."

She kicked at him furiously with her boots. "How could you be so dumb? Don't you have enough sense not to hang around in the streets? Didn't you *know* what could happen?"

"I wasn't even there! I heard the—"

"Why didn't you run home for help when your sister fell? You told your father the truth, but you never told me! Why did you hide from me all that time?"

"I didn't! I wasn't hiding, I was—"

"*Liar!*" she screamed, slapping him hard across his face. She fell to her knees again. *Why, God? Truth can kill a mother . . .*

She didn't see her son glaring down at her with loathing. She didn't hear him scrambling up the embankment. She was pulling the fog around her shoulders like a shawl. She was gripping the fence again, looking for somewhere to lie down on the other side. *She was tired, Margaret. Your Grandmother Leticia needed a place to rest.* Yes. If only she could find a place to lie down, she could let her life pass before her, see how it all began. She could find the moment when she made her first mistake. Before she married, before she had children, before she became this woman she never wanted to be.

"I'm tired, too," she murmured to her mother, to her husband, to her son.

Nobody answered.

She raised her head. The sound of a boy running down a driveway was a sound as natural as a waterfall.

"I hate you!" the boy was sobbing as he ran. "I hate you, I hate you, I hate you!"

———

"Margaret?" Bootsey called from the birdbath. "Is your hand supposed to be raised? Are you voting?"

No. I wasn't voting. I was threading my way through the chairs to reach the door into Idavillea. At the moment the draft dodgers became the official civic project of the Buckhead Garden Club, I was in Arnold Matthews's study, rifling through the drawers of his desk. I was in the kitchen helping Harold prepare another round of Perrier and Chivas Regal. I was following him out the front door and around the side of the house hidden from the patio and down the path that led to the toolshed.

"It doesn't seem possible," I said when Harold showed me the ladder. "It's too short to reach all the way up to the top of the roof."

"No, ma'am. I does it in pieces. First, I climb a piece to the ledge above them fancy columns. Then I pull that piece up over the dining room, and then I pull it over Little Arnold's bedroom, and then I push it up to the weather vane."

"And is it true what Mrs. Matthews said this afternoon?" I asked, picking up one end of the ladder. "Can you really see all the way to downtown Atlanta?"

"Yes, ma'am. Can't see it good, but you can see it kind of ghostie."

After we'd settled ourselves next to the chimney, I searched the skyline for a Sabattier effect, for a silhouette, an angle, a movement, for anything at all that would serve as a memento of my past, as a talisman for my future.

Four stories below us, the ladies of the Buckhead Garden Club had ended their meeting.

"Well! If that isn't just *like* her to climb up on a roof?" they were saying as they raced each other down the driveway.

"Always exaggerating her miseries!" they agreed as they sped away from Arcadia Heights.

"Have you *ever?*" they cried as they hurried into their houses to be the first to spread the news.

"Oh, it didn't surprise me one little bit," they whispered over their telephones to every single person in Atlanta. "I'm afraid it's exactly the kind of thing Margaret Hunter Bridges has been doing all her *life.*"

And while they were whispering, I was raising my plastic wine glass in a tribute to Harold and to the hundreds of daffodils and tulips and spiky blue flowers around the swimming pool and patio in Ida's backyard. " 'Spring, the Sweet Spring!' " I said.

"Yes, *ma'am.*"

"What?" I asked, at the sound of his chuckle.

"Excuse me. But I be remembering the sight of you marching out of Mister Matthews's study, Miz Margaret. Be wondering what that man going to say when he sees how you done messed up his desk."

"Don't worry about it. Mr. Matthews should have enough sense not to try to hide a Christmas present in the back of a drawer underneath a stack of bank deposit slips. I'll have you know, Harold, I bought this journal for him myself. It cost over one hundred dollars—"

"Uh-huh. Real leather, I see that, Miz Margaret. Got his name in gold on the cover."

"—and he never bothered to even take it out of the box!"

"Yes, ma'am," Harold answered, still chuckling. "Mister Matthews's going to fire you and me both. And I be thinking about them garden club ladies, that fat one with the snakes, the one what be so mad at you. When we was pulling the ladder up to the landing, she keep saying, 'Has you ever?' She ain't never, she say, in her whole entire life."

"That was Mrs. Johnson. You remember her, she's Mrs. Kennedy's twin sister. And those things that looked like snakes were Mrs. Kennedy's draft dodgers."

"Uh-huh. Be wearing them snakes around her neck and saying the whole time we be climbing from the landing to the roof above Little Arnold's room, 'What on earth is that idiot woman going to do next?' Huh. Miz Johnson ain't never going to climb herself up on no roof."

"True. But for her sister's sake, I wish now I'd stayed at the meeting long enough to have voted. If I'd been able to visualize in my mind's eye even one single boy from downtown Atlanta trying to protect his mother by placing a tube of cotton on her windowsill, Harold, I would most certainly have cast my vote in the affirmative."

"That's right," Harold said sadly, pointing to my bedroom window across the street. "A boy ought to protect his mama."

"One!" Ida began counting.

Cold doth not sting, the pretty birds do sing . . .

"Two!"

To witta woo . . .

I opened my journal and started writing.

In the beginning was Katherine . . .

Katherine begat Margaret, Margaret begat Minevah, Minevah begat Leticia, Leticia begat Charlotte, Charlotte begat me . . .

12

I begat Margaret Leticia Bridges.

We called her Meg . . .

She was conceived behind the closed door of a bedroom in a roach-infested apartment near the Emory University School of Law.

"It sounds gross," she said one evening at the dinner table when I was telling her some of the facts of life. "You mean married people do something like that even when they're not making a baby?"

"Jesus H. Christ, Margaret!" her father said. "Do you have to talk so dirty in front of the children?"

But Meg and I talked about many things.

"Why did Daddy's daddy die?" she asked me.

"He was very old and very tired," Peter answered from the doorway. He came over to her bed and tucked her in. "It was time for him to go live with the angels in heaven."

"Your father's a brilliant man, darling," I said the next morning when she asked again, "but unfortunately he can never tell whether he believes what he says or not. He's an agnostic. As for me, I don't know why your grandfather had to die, Meg, but you must be very sweet to your Grandmother Bridges when she comes for Thanksgiving. She's afraid nobody needs her."

"Why was Mrs. Frawley's son born nuts?" Meg asked after

Bubba Frawley, aged twenty-seven, escaped from his house one day and wandered into our yard to show little Jimmy his penis.

"Don't use the word 'nuts,'" Peter corrected from behind his newspaper. "Bubba is mentally ill. He needs sound professional care in an institution."

"I don't know why he was born that way," I said. "Just keep out of his way without hurting his feelings and don't worry about him, dear. As a group, insane people are often happier than you and I. Many actually enjoy being insane."

"Good grief," Peter groaned. "Another quote from that nut Dale Carnegie." He looked over at Meg, who was lying on the den floor crayoning a pig in a coloring book. "Your mother's completely off her rocker on that one, I'm afraid. But let's not say anything about it. We might hurt her feelings."

Meg had plenty to say about my advice on Bubba Frawley, however, and she had plenty to say later about some of my other advice:

Little girls who never frown or raise their voices, and who go out of their way to be adorable to every single solitary soul they meet, grow up to be mealymouthed and manipulative, with a tendency toward migraines.

It is wrong not to ever make fun of your friends, especially if the friends are Lucie Earle, chattering on about who deserves to be popular in your crowd, and Wally Junior, smirking over dirty jokes about homosexuals.

Stop worrying about whether or not you're being yourself. Logic teaches us it is impossible to always be ourselves because sometimes we don't know who we are, and other times we need to try to be somebody better.

As the oldest, you should try to be kind to your brother and not whine or be jealous. Even though a daddy loves both of his children, sometimes a daddy has been programmed to believe that only a boy child deserves advantages. That's why it can take a long, long time for a girl child with advantages to figure out what to do with them. But never mind, Meg. You can grow up to be anything you want to be. You have your whole life ahead of you. You don't have to be like your mother, who never had any options when she was your age.

"Oh, Meg!" I wailed. "Sometimes your mother thinks she never had any options in her whole entire *life!*"

———

" 'Socrates, the famous gadfly of Athens,' " her grandfather had read to me at the breakfast table the morning after her Uncle Buford had run away from home, " 'was a brilliant old man in spite of the fact that he went barefooted and married a girl of nineteen when he was baldheaded and forty . . .' "

I looked over at Daddy. Baldheaded. Forty. And never once, while I was screaming and slamming doors in reaction to my mother's sighs and pages of *Mrs. Dull's Guide to Southern Etiquette*, had I told him to his face he was wrong.

"I hate Daddy," I'd said to Mother the night before, when we found Buford's note stuck in her vanity mirror. ("I'm not coming back until I can cram a million dollars up his nose.")

"Don't be stupid," she'd said, almost to herself. We were in the bathroom, searching through the medicine cabinet for Daddy's tube of Ben-Gay. Looking in the cabinet under the sink for his box of Serutan ("Natures spelled backwards"), the laxative Buford said looked like rabbit shit. "Your brother ought to be able to understand how to deal with his father by now."

"But Daddy didn't have to hurt his feelings. He didn't have to make Buford feel like a fool. What difference does it make if he goes to Duke instead of Georgia Tech? Why doesn't Daddy let *me* inherit the Hunter Baking Company if Buford doesn't want it?"

"And now, *you*," Mother said, ignoring my questions. "It's bad enough when a boy rejects his father, but a *daughter!*" She looked at me in distress and then headed toward the den, where Daddy was suffering his ulcer and his migraine on the sofa with a wet rag over his forehead. Her stride slowed to a tiptoe as she neared the doorway. She whispered: "Why do you deliberately try to upset your father so? If you know what's good for you, you'll march right in there and apologize."

"I'm not going to say I'm sorry. I'm not."

Mother sighed. "I'm going to end up in a loony bin."

"This *is* a loony bin."

She gripped my arm. "If you want to blame somebody, Sister, blame yourself. If you'd kept your mouth shut, if you hadn't gone tattling to your daddy about that stupid ESP teacher and what Buford said about the Hunter Baking Company, none of this would have happened. It would have all blown over."

"*Aggghhhh,*" Daddy groaned from the den sofa that night.

" 'He sharply changed the whole course of human thought,' " Daddy was reading the next morning about this Socrates fellow, who was now honored as one of the greatest winners of friends and influencers of people our poor wrangling world had ever known. "And do you know why?" Daddy asked, interrupting his reading to fix his daughter with an earnest eye. "He was a forgiving man. He never found fault with other people, Margaret, he never told them they were wrong. Unlike a certain brother of yours I could mention, old Socrates was smart enough to know that nothing good ever comes from criticism. He always looked for the best in himself and others."

"Yes, sir."

"If Buford hadn't been in such a hurry to run away from his troubles, he could have learned to use the method the gadfly of Athens used." Daddy leaned back in his chair. "The Socratic Method, Margaret."

"Socratic, Daddy? Would that be named for Mister Socrates?"

"Of *course* it was named for Mister Socrates! Who else would it be named for?"

"Yes, sir."

"When people were mistaken, Margaret, Socrates used this

method of asking questions until he could get them to see the light. He would force them into answering his questions with a *yes*. He would keep asking questions and asking questions and forcing his opponents to answer *yes!* until, before they knew it, they were embracing the correct conclusion which only minutes earlier they had angrily denied. Do you understand what I'm telling you, Margaret?"

"No."

Daddy ground his Pall Mall out on his plate and planned his next strategy. "You don't care about how to trick people into agreeing with you?"

"No."

"Into forcing them to see the best in themselves and others?"

"No."

"You're telling me you don't want to strive for a world of *yeses*? You're sitting there, Miss Priss, in all your teenage ignorance, telling me you don't agree with the famous gadfly of Athens?"

"No."

"You think Mr. Carnegie is an idiot, don't you? Is that it? This man made billions off this book! And yet you're trying to tell me he's *wrong*?"

"No."

"What's gotten into you and your brother?" Daddy howled. "You ought to be getting down on your hands and knees every night of your life and thanking God for all the advantages you've received. Are you slouching there and telling your own father you are blind to the importance of something as basic and simple to understand as forgiveness of sins? As respect for the other fellow's inadequate point of view?"

"No."

"So!" Daddy raged. "You don't think we should all try to get along in this wrangling old world, huh? You think you're the only one who knows what is right. That's *exactly* what you think, isn't it, Miss Priss?"

"No."

"*Charlotte?*" Daddy slammed his fists on the table. "There's no talking to your daughter anymore. She's suddenly Little Miss Know-It-All. If she really thinks she knows it all, I'd like to see her twenty or thirty years from now when she has children of her own. She'll find out. Yes. That will be mighty, mighty interesting. She'll discover what it's like when her own flesh and blood turn against her. When her own child shoves a world of No! in her face instead of a world of Yes!

"Now, Walter. Calm down. You don't want to make yourself sick. Just continue with your little story, dear."

"Aghhhhh!"

Daddy hurled Mr. Carnegie's book across the room.

"I'm never going to read her anything again. No! She's so young and full of herself, she thinks she knows it all!"

———

No. I sat on a rooftop, watching my yardman clean out the gutters, and I knew there was something I'd meant to do before I came to the end of my past. I'd meant to call my daddy on the telephone and confess I knew almost nothing.

"Most of the things I do know," I'd meant to tell him, "you taught me. Remember? How to play mumbley-peg? How to make a rabbit out of a man's handkerchief? How to tell the difference between an Indian arrowhead and an ordinary piece of quartz?"

"Preserve the right mental attitude," he used to urge me. Courage, frankness, and good cheer. "We are the gods of the chrysalis," he said.

Yes. The gods of the chrysalis. It wasn't his fault that some gods got trapped inside their cocoons. That even gods like Walter James Hunter could emerge stunted, deformed, condemned to sit all day in an old red leather armchair, looking out at the world with eyes that could no longer ask or answer questions.

"Yes!" I should have said that day last year when I picked up the telephone and heard the sound of an animal growling in my ear. "Sogghhh . . . soggghhh . . ."

"Yes, Daddy," I should have told him. "I'm sorry about Meg, too."

But I was even angrier at the world that morning than I had been when I was sixteen, sitting at a breakfast table listening to a story about Socrates being read with the earnestness of Edward R. Murrow.

"Don't give me the details," I'd said to Peter the night before. "My daughter has been dead a week. Isn't that enough for a mother to know?"

———

She was only *seventeen*!

When she was two, she'd almost died of pneumonia. When she was nine, she'd almost gotten run over by a truck. When she was twelve, she'd almost drowned in a boating accident at Lake Burton.

"Well," Ida used to say, "Meg may be as sassy and as headstrong and as emotional as her mother, but you'll never have to worry about her, Margaret. Trust me. If there's one thing you've raised your daughter to be, it's a survivor."

Before her funeral, our house was filled with neighbors and friends streaming in to bring us food and words of love and condolence. "A terrible thing," they kept saying. "You are in our hearts and prayers."

But to me it was as if the terrible thing had happened to someone else. Surely it couldn't be real that the child they were grieving for was Meg!

At the gravesite, the minister of the Buckhead Presbyterian Church read a eulogy: Meg was a senior at Calvin Academy. In the fall she was to have entered Wellesley. Her favorite singer was Paul Simon. Her favorite sport was tennis. Her favorite poet was e. e. cummings. "Let us rejoice!" he said. "For in our Father's house are many mansions. Let us praise our Lord!" he said. "For as true believers, we shall surely be with Meg again one day."

No. It wasn't real. I was grieving, yes. But I was grieving for some other child than Meg. I was grieving for the nine-year-old boy whose body had been discovered on the other side of town behind an office complex three days earlier. I was grieving for some other mother than myself, some other father than Peter, some other brother than Jimmy.

I wanted to explain to the minister, who had stopped by the house the night Meg's body was transferred from the city morgue to Patterson's Funeral Home, that he shouldn't have sat in my den talking to me about eulogies. He should have been in southwest Atlanta, consoling the poor mother whose picture had been on the front page of the *Atlanta Journal* that evening, her mouth twisted in a piercing wail.

"Let not your heart be troubled," the minister had said as he sat beside me on the sofa. He took my hands in his. "Your daughter is with her Lord in heaven, according to God's predestined plan. Let us pray."

But I could not follow the sense of the prayers of a man who believed God's predestined plan included a madman who was going about killing little children and hiding their bodies under kudzu. I could not listen to a man who believed in a Jesus who suffered little children to come unto Him, who was conceived by the Holy Ghost, born of the Virgin Mary, was crucified and buried so he could rise to judge the quick and the dead.

I no longer believed in the forgiveness of sins, the life everlasting, amen.

When the minister left, I locked the front door and went upstairs to find Jimmy. He was lying on his back on top of Meg's four-poster bed. It was the same bed I'd slept in when I was a little girl and my mother had come into my room to tell me my grandmother had gone to heaven.

I lay down beside my child, as my own mother had done before me, but I did not speak. Jimmy and I did not mention Meg or Meg's father, who was at the funeral home making the arrangements. We said not a word about the way her grandfather had come out of the woods the day before with feet that could barely shuffle and hands that would never again grab the world by its throat until it hollered yes.

Jimmy and I lay very still. Perhaps we slept. At some point during the night, Peter came home.

"I took them the white dress Meg was supposed to wear to graduation," he said, laying down beside me. "They told me there was a button missing."

I did not answer. There was nothing to say. "Dear God," I prayed. And other things I prayed. But not out loud. Out loud, I sat up in bed and waited.

After a long time I whispered, "Meg?"

The room was silent.

After a long, long time I lay my head back on Peter's shoulder and I closed my eyes to wait some more.

And one year later, as I sat on a rooftop watching the curtains in my bedroom window across the street being pulled closed by my son, I realized I was still . . .

Waiting.

———

"Why is Debbie Sue Regenstein going to hell after she grows up and dies?" Meg had asked when she was seven.

"Ah, Meg. Don't listen to every little thing somebody at Sunday School tells you," I'd answered, looking up from the book I was reading to Jimmy in my lap. "There is no such place as hell. If it were so, I would have told you."

"Why did you lie to Jimmy and me when we were little? Why did you tell us the possums in the street were only sleeping?"

"For crying out loud, Meg! Can't you see I'm trying to read this book to Jimmy? Leave us alone and stop asking me why all the time."

"Read it again!" Jimmy demanded.

"All right," I said, "but this is the very last time."

"But why?" he cried, when I got to the end. "Why does the mother have to die?"

"The mushroom was poisonous," Meg explained patiently, taking the book out of my hand and flipping to the second page. "Babar's mother found it in the forest and she ate it and it killed her dead."

"No!" Jimmy cried. "Read it again."

"Why don't you let me do it for him, Mom?" Meg said calmly. "I know how to read it so the mother doesn't die."

———

Margaret Leticia Bridges. She'd owned seventeen music boxes. She'd owned a doll that could tell a story by her favorite poet in the voice of her great-grandmother:

> "I've come from the fartherest star to tell you that you've got to stop this why-ing."
> "Why," said the little very very very old man.
> At this, the faerie grew pink with anger. "If you don't stop asking why," he said, "you'll be sorry."
> "Why?" said the little very very old man.
> "Now see here," the faerie said. "If you say why again, you'll fall from the moon all the way to the earth."
> And the little very old man smiled; and looking at the faerie, he said "why?" and he fell millions and millions of deep cool new beautiful miles (and with every part of a mile he became a little younger; first he became a not very old man and next a middle-aged man and finally a child) until, just as he gently touched the earth, he was about to be born.

Part Four

Sunset in Arcadia Heights. As I close my journal, a deep orange spills from the sky and begins spreading slowly over the roof. I study its progress until it has covered the piles of dead leaves and red-clay slime that Harold and I removed from the gutters this afternoon and arranged like graffiti across Arnold's antique cedar shingles.

Arcadia Heights is quiet now, preparing for the end of day. No buzz saws, no birds chirping, no trucks grinding their way up the access road. Harold is asleep by the chimney. I can smell the dinner Ida is cooking: fried chicken, turnip greens, probably rice and gravy. If she and Arnold have any idea I am still on top of their house, they gave no indication of it when they arrived home a few minutes ago. Before she followed her husband into Idavillia, Ida slammed her tennis racket against a lawn chair and then threw it across the patio in a way that let me know the Buckhead Bombers had just been eaten alive by the Arcadia Heights Harpies.

I don't need to look across the street to know that Jimmy is no longer at my bedroom window. But I look anyway, just to make sure. I did not see him when he left for the lake with his father, but I can picture the two of them ambling across the lawn toward Peter's new red Jaguar parked at the curb. Peter would have had his arm around Jimmy's shoulder. When they reached the car, he would have tossed the keys to his son and laughed. If he paused to look up at the woman sitting on a roof beside her old yardman, it would not have occurred to him to run across the street and save her. I'm beginning to realize that Peter has barely enough strength to save himself.

I turn away from my house and begin crawling to the other side of the roof. In the distance, the skyline of Atlanta looks . . .

"Ghostie," I conceded to Harold this afternoon.

"Yes, *ma'am!*" he agreed.

While we were spreading the gutter debris across the roof, I told him about going downtown two days ago to sign the separation agreement with Peter. About the huge hole in the ground where HARDINGS WAS HERE!

"There was red clay mud and water flowing like blood down the street," I told him. "As I made my way toward the Davison's parking lot, I felt like I was evacuating a war zone. I kept looking for what was missing in action."

The Coca-Cola sign was missing. The Loew's Grand and Paramount theaters. Leon Froshin's, J. P. Allen, Maier & Berkele Jewelers, the Henry Grady Hotel. Missing. The Lane Rexall Drugstore and the Francis Virginia Tea Room on the third floor above Lane Rexall. Also missing . . .

"Ain't much left of old Atlanta," Harold said. "I likes the new Atlanta even better, don't you?"

"Ah, yes," I answered bitterly. "The City Too Busy to Hate."

"The Next Great *International* City, Miz Margaret!"

I made no comment. Harold was the last person on earth I should have allowed to come up on the roof with me. And I was having trouble making him leave.

"Go home," I said, trying once more to convince him to walk over to my house and find money for a taxi in my pocketbook. "If you don't get there before your dinner is cold, Earllovette will be furious with you."

"Why, I can't leave you up here by yourself, Miz Margaret! You knows better than to ask me to do a thing like that!"

"I may stay all night," I told him angrily. "You really want to stay up here all night?"

He grinned. "Now, Miz Margaret. You ain't really going to do that. You just being stubborn."

"You wait and see."

Yes. I am almost to the end of my past. In another hour it will be dark and I can leave my journal behind for somebody else's future.

Jimmy's.

THREE LAST THINGS
I WISH I'D DONE

1. *Sewn the button on Meg's dress.*
2. *Brought Peter to his knees.*
3. *Hugged my son good-bye and told him . . .*

Told him what?

How does a mother begin to list all the missed opportunities, the misguided intentions? Even if she knows where to begin, how can she explain the ending so her child will understand and forgive her?

Is it enough to have written down stories of when I was a little girl? Should I have also told him about the stories I used to make up when I was playing in the woods across the street with my brother and my friends? Tried to explain to my son that his mother had actually *believed* those stories? Had believed if I learned to kiss my elbow I would turn into a boy like Buford and get to build Indian tepees and smoke rabbit tobacco and play on the Civil War cannon in the creek bed? Had believed if I were very, very good to everyone I met I would get to grow up and marry a man like my daddy and live in a house like my mother's house and have children who would someday make me a grandmother like my Grandmother Leticia?

What kinds of stories did Jimmy tell himself that afternoon in the woods while he hid beside his sister's body?

What kinds of stories is he telling himself now?

I swing my legs over the edge of the roof and look down on the cars that are making their slow escape from downtown Atlanta. Yes! Try to get away! HARDINGS HAS COME! HARDINGS HAS COME!

My words race across the page in slanted, urgent lines to reach the end of my journal:

STORIES FOR MY SON

They may have attempted to ape the customs of southern breeding, dear heart, but they made a total mockery of it in the process. . . . Poor Mom. You're still the same old Buckhead pink you were before you married Dad. . . . Even though Jesus loves all the little children, Margaret, and suffers them to come unto Him, Jesus decided not to give some of the little children Grace before they were born, so they are predestined to burn eternally in Hell after they grow up and die. . . . Why do you always expect the worse, Mom? I told you everything would turn out all right. . . . Ha! Ha! Ha! Once a boy finds out he's going to be a cripple, he becomes happier than normal boys. . . . Look around you, Margaret! Everything is old and dying. We live in a goddamned crypt! . . . If you're not going to be a good sport, I'll just drive you back to your car. Honestly! You used to be fun, you used to be downright insane. . . . When are you going to learn, Margaret, that when something unpleasant is happening, you must pretend not to notice? . . . The City Too Busy to Hate. . . . The Next International City, Miz Margaret. . . . Hush, baby. You is the cryingest child I ever did see . . .

I slam my journal shut.

"I like the new Atlanta even better than the old one," Harold had said. "Don't you?"

No. I should never have invited him to come on the roof with me. He's an old fool. And for what had I been hoping? For him to save me?

Then I am as big a fool as he is. Because I should know by now that all kinds of moral and sociological issues are involved. Can a person save somebody who doesn't want to be saved? What if the person who doesn't want to be saved is a woman, and the person who might or might not try to save her is a man? Does that make a difference anymore?

And then, of course, there is the added complication of race and class. Does a poor black person have a responsibility toward a rich white person? Shouldn't that be the other way around?

But it would take a miracle for either one of us to change at this late date. The sad truth of age is not that we become older and wiser, but that we become more than ever who we have always been. Under my grown-up pioneer skirt and blouse is simply a more intense version of the child I'd been when I wore a yellow sundress and sat in my maid's lap crying because my brother wasn't being nice to me, of the teenage girl in a poodle skirt I had been that morning at the breakfast table when I rebelled against Socrates and my father.

Yes, despite all the changes of these past twenty years, beneath Harold's black skin is the same subservient young man who used to drive a bakery wagon through Buckhead, yes-ma'aming and no-ma'aming all the white ladies.

"What would your daddy think if he knew I was leaving you alone up here?" Harold asked when I ordered him to take the MARTA bus home. "What your mama say?"

"I'm not a child," I told him angrily.

"Well, you'll always be a child to them," he answered. "And you be a child to me," he said when I ordered him to go across the street and get taxi money from Jimmy. "Same sassy little girl you was when I used to have to let you climb up on my bakery wagon. Uh-huh. 'Let her do it,' I say to myself. 'Because until she do it, you ain't never going to be able to get these rolls delivered.'"

I begin crawling back up to the chimney. Yes, he's an old fool. And if I don't get him off of here soon, it will be too late. Too dark for an old fool to climb down a ladder.

"Harold," I order, nudging his prone body with my boot. "Wake up."

He groans.

I squat down beside him. "Come on, Harold."

He knocks my hand away with his arm.

I look at his stubborn, flaccid face and it suddenly occurs to me that his skin is not actually black at all; it's the color of dark chocolate. The scar, which begins below his right ear and runs in a ragged line along the edge of his jaw before making a turn at his chin and slashing down across his Adam's apple, has the sheen of . . . satin. It ends just below the collar of his shirt.

The shirt, I know, is from Brooks Brothers. Pink Oxford cloth and monogrammed with my almost ex-husband's initials. It has been ironed, no doubt, by Harold's wife, Earllovette—a woman who looks (according to Harold) like a cross between the way Pearl Bailey talks and the way Lena Horne sings.

I lean over his chest and listen to his wheezy snore. I smell his boozy breath. His khaki trousers are worn at the knees. His broken fingernails are caked with red clay and slime from the gutters. And when did he become so old?

"Please, Harold," I whisper. "Get up."

I stand in order to get a better view at him. If one squints one's eyes . . .

I try to visualize him as white. He is tall and rangy, like Jimmy Stewart, maybe. Not as Jimmy Stewart looked in the movies, but Jimmy Stewart as he looks today, distinguished by age. And then I begin to see a certain resemblance to the other Jimmy Stewart, too. The one in *The Philadelphia Story*, carrying Katharine Hepburn in his arms one early morning when they both are very, very tired. Or Jimmy as Charles Lindbergh, flying over the Atlantic alone, exhausted, with only a fly for company.

"Ah, Harold," I whisper. "I'm sorry about your worn trousers and your filthy fingernails. I'm sorry about all those little children of your race who are going around being murdered."

He does not say a word against me.

"Yes, I'm sorry," I will tell after I wake him up. "I meant to be a different woman. I was supposed to be a heroine and save you, Harold. But those were other times, back then. And you have to understand it was not my fault. The world is full of needs. You and yours are not the only ones. No! If I had gone on a Freedom Ride through Alabama, I would have been kicked out of Sweet Briar. And later . . . why, I had little *children* to look after!"

Harold moans in his dreams. He stinks of scotch and sweat and cow manure. His nose is broad. His lips are wide. His bald head is as round as a melon.

"And let me tell you something else," I whisper angrily. "Just because I'm white doesn't mean I'm supposed to spend my entire life making up for everything my Atlanta ancestors did to your people before I was even *born!*"

He wheezes like a mule.

I kneel down on the roof.

"Ah, Harold," I whisper in his ear so he can hear me. "There's one last thing I need to do before it's too late. I need to tell you I'm sorry."

Yes. I grab the white butler's jacket from Ida's weather vane and lay it across Harold's chest so he won't look so cold.

"Oh, Harold Booker Washington! All my life I've meant to tell you I am just extremely . . . *extremely* . . . sorry."

13

"*Doric, five,*" *Ida called to me from across the aisle.*

"*Corinthian, eleven,*" *I called loudly back.*

We were showing off. The grown-ups on the bus kept scowling at us.

So what? We were fifteen-year-old Buckhead pinks, rich high school girls from Calvin Academy enjoying ourselves after a day shopping for clothes at Rich's, J. P. Allen's, and Davison's. Sassy teenagers passing the time by instructing the other passengers on the styles and numbers of columns along Peachtree Street. Already some of the fancy houses Ida and I had known since we were children had changed into office buildings and cheap hotels rented by the week. *Room and Board . . . Beware the Dog . . . Keep Out! This Property is Protected by Private Security . . .*

When the man in the bow tie boarded the bus at the corner of Ponce de Leon, I hardly noticed him. He was of no interest; he was old enough to be my daddy. But when he stopped midway down the aisle and began waving a copy of the *Atlanta Journal* above his head, I quit trying to imagine a name for the Egyptian columns on the Fox Theater and gave the man a second look.

"Tacky," I mouthed silently across the aisle to Ida.

He was wearing suspenders instead of a belt. The cuffs on his pants were too wide.

"You want I should read it out loud?" he shouted eagerly.

Murmurs. Nods. Yes, the other passengers very much wanted this man to read it out loud.

"Why, it's downright disgusting!" a man sitting in front of Ida cried out when the reading was finished.

"Nigger lovers!" another man announced. "Every single one of those judges up there is a nigger lover!"

Ida, who had been scrunched up next to her window, slid across the seat to sit by the aisle so she could get a better view of the short, chubby man who was now standing up, saying, "You get them Commies up there on the Supreme Court and the exact next thing you know, you got to send your own flesh and blood to school with pickaninnies. Colored babies!"

"And did you hear about that genius boy from Jasper, Georgia?" the lady in back of me asked. She jabbed a finger in my shoulder to make sure I was listening. "He had everything in life ahead of him until his father got transferred to Chicago and he had to go to an integrated school. All his classmates called him 'Whitey.' Why, he ended up blowing his brains out!"

"And did you hear," someone asked, "about the girl from Moultrie who was raped in Boston by a Negro with a whip?"

"With a *leather* whip!"

"And did you hear . . .?"

The stories raced through the bus. Stories of knifings and spittings and idleness. Of *sass*!

Stories of white girls having to share the Ladies Room with coloreds.

"*Syphilis.*"

Of white girls having to eat in the same school cafeteria with Ubangis.

"Worms!"

Of white girls being forced to dance at the Senior Prom with Yankee coons.

"Interracial *marriage!*"

Ida and I looked across the aisle at each other in excitement. We were witnessing a scene!

— 195 —

"Well, they'll never get away with it in Atlanta," said the man in the bow tie. "I can assure you all of that much. If they think they can come down here and tell us what to do with our own schools, they got another think coming. There's a little matter in the Constitution of the U S and A called 'States' Rights.' Next thing, I guess they'll be trying to tell us we got to integrate our churches."

The bell was ringing. Ringing again. Somebody needed to get off.

The storytellers paused. I turned around in my seat. All the colored people at the back of the bus were quietly filing out. The hands of the ones to reach the sidewalk first were solemnly raised to assist the ones who were coming after them down the steps. They were the hands of every colored person I had ever known. Hands holding a rake . . . hands guiding an iron . . . hands pouring me another cup of Ovaltine . . .

As the doors *whooshed* closed and the bus pulled away from the curb, Ida flopped down on the seat beside me and grabbed my arm. "Have you ever?" she cried excitedly. "I have absolutely *never!*"

I shook my head and stared out the window until the colored people were no longer in sight.

"Did you see them?" Ida was asking eagerly. "Can you believe the way they filed out at the same time without saying one *word?*"

I opened the window and rested my head on the sill.

"Oh, for goodness sakes!" Ida said in her Tinkerbell voice. "Stop playing like you're sick! You know as well as I do that your daddy isn't going to allow a nigra to go to school with you. I sincerely don't know what gets into you sometimes, Margaret Hunter. Sometimes you act like you don't understand anything at all."

I quit listening. And when the bus reached the edge of Buckhead and Ida pulled the cord for our stop, I didn't get off with her. I waited another block until I saw Mr. Levine standing on the sidewalk in front of his fruit emporium. I knew he would let me sit at one of his tables in the back and he would bring me a glass of crushed ice and Coca-Cola to settle my stomach. Mr. Levine would telephone my mother to come and get me.

———

"I want to talk to Beatrice," I told my mother on the way home in the car.

"Oh, Margaret," she sighed. "You fall apart over the least little thing. If you don't start responding to problems with a little more grace and dignity, you're going to drive me straight to the insane asylum."

"But it's not fair," I said.

"You don't have any idea what is fair and what is not fair. In any case, it's none of your business."

I said nothing.

"Now you listen to me, young lady. Keep your opinions to yourself. Otherwise you're going to upset your father."

But I didn't want to listen to Mother. The person I wanted to listen to was Beatrice Maxwell Jones. "Hush, baby," she'd said whenever I was angry or hurt and ran downstairs for solace to her maid's room in the basement. "Let it slide on by," she'd crooned.

I would climb on her lap and get her to sing to me in the rocking chair that had mushrooms carved into the tips of the arms.

"You is the cryingest child I ever did see," she told me that morning when I was five and I went flying downstairs in terror to find her.

Mother was *away*.

"She's got TB," my Grandmother Leticia whispered when anyone asked.

"Why, poor little thing!" the woman with the spotted veil over her face had said to me the day Grandmother Leticia took me downtown to the Francis Virginia Tea Room for lunch and let me buy a music box in Woolworth's with Snow White dancing on the lid. "Her mama's got TB."

"Imbecile!" Grandmother said as soon as the lady's back was

turned. She marched down the sidewalk, imitating the way the lady had said, "poor little thing," and the way the lady's eyebrows had lifted in disapproval when she bent down to kiss me on my forehead and then drew back suddenly in a way that let me know I was nasty.

"Common!" Grandmother said under her breath, grabbing my hand and leading me past the jewelry store and past the man who shined men's shoes and past the photography shop that had pictures of sailors pasted in the window. "A lah-de-dah imbecile from Savannah!" Grandmother said out loud, pulling me into the Lane Rexall Drugstore and ordering the man wearing the paper hat to bring us something refreshing.

"My beautiful granddaughter," she said, after kissing me firmly on the lips, "will have a Coca-Cola with a lacing of cherry syrup." She removed her black gloves and began patting the lace at her bosom. "A touch of ammonia, young man, in mine. Just a touch of *ammonia!*"

"Hush, baby," Beatrice said that morning I went flying down to her room in the basement after I'd been taken into Daddy's room to meet a ghastly pale lady who was stretched out on the chaise lounge and who was, I realized, the lady I'd had nightmares about from *The Mummy's Ghost*.

"You is the cryingest child I ever did see," Beatrice told me that morning she sat me on her lap and sang to me because the lady had held out her arms and tried to grab me. "That's your mama, child. She done come home to take your old Beatrice's place."

"I need to talk to Beatrice," I kept telling my mother for days after she came to pick me up at Mr. Levine's fruit emporium. But I didn't know where to find her. Beatrice hadn't worked for us in over a year. She'd been shot in the stomach by a crazy man, and she had taken so much medicine to ease her pain that when she tried to return to live in our basement she wasn't allowed to stay.

I didn't find her again until I was over forty years old.

All the way to Beatrice's funeral last summer, Mother reminisced about her favorite maid. "Do you remember . . .?" Mother kept asking. "And remember when . . .?"

"Yes. I remember."

"But I had to let her go, Margaret," Mother said. "I would come home from shopping or bridge and there she would be! Passed right out on your bed! Beatrice was sorely addicted, wasn't she, Walter?" Mother said, turning to Daddy. "We tried to help her. We sent her money." Then she turned back to me. "But she was sorely addicted for the longest time, Margaret."

"Yes," I said.

"It was those drugs they gave her in the hospital after she was shot, wasn't it, Walter? So there was nothing we could do. You understand, don't you, Margaret? You see now why we had to let her go?"

"Yes."

"Then when we took her back, you were at Sweet Briar, dear. And Beatrice just wasn't the same, was she, Walter? She was never quite the same."

Walter said nothing. Walter could no longer speak.

We were passing down Auburn Avenue, where Ida and I used to go with our dates to a black nightclub for rich Negroes and listen to the likes of Ella Fitzgerald and Fats Domino and an albino with red hair who played the piano.

"Still, there's never been another like Beatrice," Mother said. She pulled a white lace handkerchief out of her purse and unfolded it. She laid it across her lap like a napkin. "She was a wonderful woman," Mother said, smoothing the handkerchief with her fingers. "A marvelous cook. Those peach fried pies she could make! Remember? And a beautiful ironer . . ."

Mother held the corner of the handkerchief up to one eye, then the other. "But those were different days back then, Margaret. I used to dress you in yellow ruffled sundresses. With long sashes . . . and *smocking*! And Beatrice used to live in the downstairs bedroom and wake up every morning to fix our breakfast.

She used to wear a nylon stocking over her head and she chewed Argo Starch to lighten her skin. Well! I wouldn't expect you to remember, dear. You were only a little girl . . ."

The chapel of the funeral home was half full when we arrived. Beatrice's family overflowed the first four rows. I didn't know any of them except Duncan, Beatrice's son who used to drive me sometimes to piano lessons. Duncan hadn't been much older than I was then. Now his son was in medical school at Emory, he said. His daughter was a teacher at Morehouse College.

"We were all real sorry to read in the newspapers about your daughter," he said to me. "Mama cried like a baby."

I didn't recognize the puffy old lady lying in the satin-lined coffin. She was nobody I had ever seen.

When Duncan asked me to stand and say a few words on behalf of Mr. and Mrs. Walter Hunter and on behalf of their absent son, Buford Hunter, I was grateful for the chance. I wanted to say how much I'd loved her. "For a long time," I wanted to tell those gathered in the chapel, "I thought she was my mother."

And then I needed to say I was so dreadfully sorry, Beatrice. I needed to explain about the time I was fifteen and rode on the bus through downtown Atlanta, and how I honestly had not realized until that afternoon that the black children in the pictures on the walls of the Buckhead Presbyterian Church Sunday School room were from Georgia. I had always thought they were from Africa or China. And when we sang—and I *believed* the words we sang— that red or yellow, black or white, they are precious in His sight, it never occurred to me or to the Sunday School teachers or to my mother who was secretary of the Women's Bible Circle, or to my daddy who was a deacon and the president of the Men's Berean Bible Class, that we were singing about Atlanta black people.

The black people we were singing about were not Beatrice, who, on Sundays and Maid's Night Out, lived in a shack set up on stilts above a red clay yard. They were not Mozel, our yardman, or Harold, the man who drove a Hunter Baking Company wagon behind a horse through our Buckhead neighborhoods. They were not Flossie May, the carhop at The Varsity, who made his money grinning and shuffling for the Buckhead Good Old Boys who paid him extra tips for wearing silly hats and screaming out the complete menu at the top of his lungs. The blacks on the walls of my Sunday School class couldn't possibly have been kin to Blind Willie McTell, the man behind the Blue Lantern drive-in on Ponce de Leon Avenue who wasted his talents on a twelve-string guitar playing for nickels and swigs of Pabst Blue Ribbon beer . . .

Except for the low organ music reaching us through a hidden speaker in the ceiling, the funeral chapel was hushed when I rose from my pew to say a few words on behalf of the Hunter family. No "amens!" No fans with pictures of Jesus being waved in front of swooning, hysterical women.

Those gathered together in the chapel to say good-bye to Beatrice Maxwell Jones, mother of Duncan and Bates and Mandie and Roberta, grandmother to a row or two of grown children, great-grandmother to the baby crying in the fourth pew, were waiting patiently for my words to come.

I waited, too. But as I stood there, I couldn't seem to nudge my mind beyond the memory of the last time I'd seen Beatrice.

"So," I finally said out loud, looking down at the moist handkerchief my mother still gripped in her lap. "The last time I ever saw Beatrice Jones was on a morning in late August, a few days before she decided it was time to retire and quit working for the Hunter family. And so . . ."

My mind stuck on the memory and began playing it back to me as though it were telling me a story.

"And, so, then . . .," I heard myself saying out loud in my Buckhead pink voice, in my Southern Belle voice, my dumb-as-they-come voice strangled by years of living in the Next Great International City, the Dogwood City, the City Too Busy to Hate. My throat closed to the size of a drinking straw. My tongue swelled to the roof of my mouth.

I looked over at Duncan. "I'm sorry . . ."

I looked around the chapel at Beatrice's family and friends.

"I'm just terribly, terribly sorry," I murmured over the sound of the story playing in my head.

So the last time I ever saw Beatrice Maxwell Jones, I had just returned from my honeymoon and I went over to Mother and Daddy's house to pick up some of the wedding presents that had arrived while Mr. Bridges and I were at Sea Island . . .

And so, Mother and I were in the living room, unwrapping a sterling silver nutmeg grater, when it occurred to Mother that she would need to explain to Beatrice that now that I was a married woman it was no longer correct for her to call me by my first name.

And so then, Mother asked Beatrice to come into the living room, and she said: "Beatrice, I'd like you to meet Mrs. Bridges."

And Beatrice stopped dead in her tracks. "You don't mean it, Missus Hunter!" she said. She tiptoed over to me and stared me down. Then she turned back to Mother.

I sank into my pew, feeling sick and ashamed. I was a fifteen-year-old girl stepping down off a bus and running into Mr. Levine's fruit emporium to wait for her mother to come and take her home.

"Lord Jesus, Missus Hunter!" Beatrice cried angrily, going into her old Aunt Jemima act: hands on face, eyes rolling. "But don't that girl look just exactly like my very own Margaret?"

14

"Remember Mr. Levine's fruit emporium?" I ask Harold when he finally awakens.

"No, ma'am."

"Across the street from E. Rivers School? And everybody in Atlanta used to go there for watermelons during the summer?"

When he doesn't answer, I lay my head back against the chimney and sigh with regret and shame. No, of course not. He wouldn't remember.

The sky is dark. Starless. But above my house across the street the moon is as orange as the pumpkins Mr. Levine used to stack beside the door of the back room. The floor was covered in thick sawdust. The walls were made of screens. On summer nights when I was growing up, my mother and father and Buford and I would sit at one of the long wooden tables and order a watermelon from the piles arranged along two sides of the room.

"Well, Benny," Daddy would say. "You're the expert. We'll leave the choosing to you."

And Mr. Levine, wearing an apron with a fountain pen clipped to the pocket, would laugh and walk over to a pile. He'd eye the watermelons, pick up one or two, and then thump them with his knuckles. "No," he'd mutter. He'd keep shaking his head until he found the one he liked. "I got us a good one," he'd say then, slicing it on the newspapers spread over the top of our table.

Mother would carefully divide her slice into neat squares. She'd remove the seeds daintily with her fork and lay them in a row beside her. I would pick the seeds out with my fingers, Buford would spit his on the sawdust floor, and Daddy would take the whole slice up to his mouth, biting and spitting seeds and talking all at the same time. He would laugh and speak to everybody else who was in the back room with us, introducing us by name to the strangers sitting at the other tables. Telling tales on Benny Levine. Cracking jokes and asking questions of these strangers until Mother would nudge him in his side and whisper, "Walter! *Hush!* Try to show a little grace and dignity!"

But Daddy loved these strangers. He loved to laugh and ask them all about themselves and tell them all about his own family. His daughter Margaret, who was going to grow up to be a concert pianist. His son Buford, who was going to take over the Hunter Baking Company from his old man one day. And Charlotte, his wife. Wasn't she a pretty thing? You'd never guess to look at her, would you, that she almost died in a sanitarium with tuberculosis?

By the end of the summer there would be no more strangers in the back room of Mr. Levine's emporium. There would be Sam and Katie and their children, Matthew and Mark and Luke and Sarah. There would be old Mr. Rosenbaum, the man Buford and I caught one night urinating into a bush behind the screen. There would be Charlie and Clyde, who lived together in an apartment on Peachtree Road and who fed their cat Millicent watermelon rinds.

"There were names and faces and stories and laughter that now, after thirty years, I can no longer remember," I tell Harold. "But, oh! The smell of those watermelons! The smell of those pumpkins ripening by the door!"

"Yes, ma'am."

I look over at him. It occurs to me that my favorite smells on an April night in the suburbs are a combination of Chivas Regal, sweat, and cow manure. My favorite sight is a pink Oxford-cloth shirt from Brooks Brothers, monogrammed with my husband's initials and ironed beautifully by a woman who looks like a cross between the way Pearl Bailey talks and Lena Horne sings. My favorite sound is a chuckle.

"What now?" I ask.

"Excuse me," he answers. "I just be thinking about what Earllovette going to say when she find out I be spending the night up on Mrs. Matthews's roof."

"I'm sorry, Harold. I should have made you get down in time to catch the MARTA bus."

"No, *ma'am*. I *enjoys* new experiences!"

Yes. This will probably be the first time in Harold's whole entire life he's ever spent all night on a roof with a Magnolia Honkie. Because it is too late now. He is too infirm to climb down by himself when it is dark. And too old, I think sadly but with gratitude, to change.

"We're two anachronisms," I would like to tell Harold. "Two products of the same dying culture." Instead, I apologize to him about Earllovette. "At this very moment, she's probably waiting supper for you, Harold. She's probably worried about you. Tell her I'm sorry when you see her."

"Yes, ma'am."

I close my eyes and try to visualize Earllovette on all those nights when her husband returns from Arcadia Heights after having worked all day for Ida and me. Before she allows him to sit down at her nice clean table, she'll have to make him change his clothes, of course. Wash his face and hands. Scrub the red clay from under his fingernails. And he, in turn, will make her wait for his words of praise—"Uh-huh"—until he's finished rolling a bite of greens over his tongue and mopped up the pot liquor with a wedge of her cornbread.

"Thank you for staying with me, Harold."

"Yes, ma'am."

"Do you think she'll be mad?" I ask.

"Earllovette?" He drops his head back against the chimney and laughs. "Miz Margaret, living with that woman be like living with Muhammad Ali. One minute she float like a butterfly, next minute she sting like a bee."

———

Other stories for my son:

When your mother was three, she learned to count on her fingers by chanting, "Eenie, Meenie, Minee, Mo; Catch a nigger by its toe."

When she was seven, she lost a nickel after her maid, Beatrice, bet her she wouldn't have enough nerve to drink from a fountain for colored people.

When your mother was twelve, she won a school contest sponsored by the Chamber of Commerce for an essay entitled: "My Favorite Traditions in Atlanta: The Gateway City of the South."

"Listen to me, Jimmy!" I want to scream to the empty house across the street. "This woman sitting on the edge of a roof, writing stories for you, is not the lapsed Southern Belle you think she is!"

No. Who she is, I wish I could explain to my son, is just a frightened and confused fifteen-year-old girl on her way home from downtown Atlanta . . .

Ten o'clock. Do you know where your children are?

It is cold on the roof. Dark and lonely. The Matthewses have turned off the evening news and gone to bed. Harold is curled up beside the chimney, sleeping again. And on the highway below, cars are speeding in both directions now, their headlights streaking through the night like flares. But it is too late for warnings. My flashlight is already aimed at the last page of my journal.

Dear Mother,

No crime has been committed here. For some of us, the stories of our lives unfold by accident . . .

A siren is screaming somewhere off in the night.

It would have taken a miracle for us to have turned out differently . . .

Yes. There is always a siren screaming somewhere off in the night.

— 206 —

Look, Margaret! The mannequins are waving to you! . . . You is the cryingest child I ever did see. . . . Ga-lump-a-rump, Ga-lump-a-rump. . . . If you don't start behaving with a bit more grace and dignity, you're going to drive me straight to the insane asylum. . . . It's easy. You just go limp and let them drag you away. . . . Why did you lie to us when we were little? Why did you tell us the possums in the street were only sleeping? . . . Read it again! . . . Why? asked the very very little old man. And he fell millions of miles until he touched the earth and was about to be . . .

My pen pauses while I wait for . . . what? The wind is suddenly blowing the tops of the pine trees. The air is heavy with the threat of rain. I turn my head slowly around and strain to see through the darkness. Is someone walking across the roof?

Why don't you let me read it to him, Mom? I know how to read it so the mother doesn't die . . .

"Meg?" I whisper.

And even before I hear the answer, I feel it. And I know it isn't true that nobody believes in miracles anymore.

I believe in miracles.

"Oh, darling," I whisper.

The shadow is moving slowly toward me. Easy. Cocky. His father's son.

Part Five

Walter James Hunter Bridges. When he was one, he wore high-topped shoes I polished for him every day. When he was six, he insisted on sleeping in the space helmet his sister gave him for his birthday. When he was eleven, he refused to let me exchange the navy blazer his grandfather had bought him in size 14.

"Trust me," my best friend said after I'd shortened the sleeves but could do nothing about the shoulders that swallowed him or the length that hung down to his thighs. "We'll find your son again in another two or three years."

When he came up on the roof he was wearing military boots and spurs. No socks. A black leather bracelet with studs.

"Mom?" he called. "What are you doing up here? Aren't you coming home?"

His voice was controlled. Private. Detached.

I could almost smell his shame as he eased down on the edge of the roof beside me. *What kind of a mother hides on top of a house? What if somebody's seen you?*

"I decided I didn't want to go to the lake, so Dad just took me to the movies. What's the matter, Mom? Are you still mad?"

Yes. I'm mad. Nuts. Off my rocker.

"But it wasn't me who caused that old guy to panic, Mom. I told you. It was Billy Ferguson."

It was Billy. Yes. It was Meg, Peter, me. It was everybody and everything that had ever been a part of my son since the day he was born. He was no more responsible for his life than the rest of us. We were all mad. All locked up in the same insane asylum.

"Jesus," he groaned. He buried his face in his fists.

I waited for the words of my accuser.

"I'm sorry, Mom."

Ah.

"You hate me because I didn't run home for help that day. But, Mom! She was already dead. I couldn't just leave her lying there all by herself, could I?"

I heard his sob. "No. You couldn't just leave her lying there all by herself."

"And I wasn't hiding from you all that time, Mom. I swear. I was *waiting* for you."

Yes.

And I was still waiting, too. For something nameless. For whatever story I'd been trying to tell my son for a long, long time.

Jimmy turned and looked at me. "Dad said you didn't want to know. He said we had to protect you. But you've known all along, haven't you, Mom?"

"Yes." *For a mother the truth is always there, lurking at the edge of her dreams, lying in wait to show her what she can't bear to see . . .*

I inhaled the black night, cradled it in my lungs.

"It was an accident!" Jimmy cried out. "I thought she was holding onto the vine!" His sob was a child's. "I didn't *mean* to push her!"

The night exploded through my chest, escaped without a sound.

———

Behind our backs, the moon shone down on the roof, marking the overlapping shingles, the piles of dead leaves, the long, curved shape of a man curled up asleep beside the chimney. Light and shadow. The Sabbatier effect.

"I would have saved her if I could," Jimmy said after a while.

I cradled his head against my shoulder. "Listen, Jimmy!" I said. "You have your whole life ahead of you, darling. You'll see. Why, ten years from now you'll be a world-famous photographer! Imagine! My son a world-*famous* photographer!"

He answered with a sob, a laugh. After a moment he twisted his head away from me and said, "So, tell me the truth. Is Dad ever coming home?"

I didn't know the truth. Instead, I told him about the night I'd fallen in love with his father. Not the details, of course. Just the way the stars had shown above us, no moon, and the way we'd sung songs around the bonfire.

"I believe for every drop of rain that falls, a flower grows," I sang to Jimmy, laughing. "I believe that even in the darkest night, a candle glows . . ."

"Aw, *Mom*," he groaned, embarrassed at my sentimental garbage.

So then I told him another story, a truer story. I told him about the time his mother looked out a bus window and saw Mr. Levine standing on the sidewalk in front of his emporium, wiping his hands on a watermelon-stained apron. And after we'd covered Harold with one of the blankets Jimmy had brought up with him, and after we'd settled ourselves again on the edge of the roof overlooking the skyline of the city, I told him the story I'd meant to tell his father just before I signed the separation agreement. The story of the night Mr. Levine leaned his elbow on our table and told us the fruit emporium was going to close. It was all over. He was selling out to the developers. They were going to clear out the woods behind the back room and change it into the Peachtree Battle Shopping Center.

A shopping center, I'd thought excitedly. Now we were finally going to be like every other city. The New York City of the South. Already most of the old houses along Peachtree Street had been torn down to make room for skyscrapers. The expressway was about to be connected all the way to downtown. Yes, everything was changing. In a few weeks I'd be marrying Peter.

"But this is family," Daddy said when Mr. Levine explained that since his wife had died he was giving up. He was moving to Jacksonville to be near his daughter.

I turned away from the look of resignation on Mr. Levine's face and turned instead toward the string of white Christmas tree lights that were strung along the outside of the screens to discourage the bugs. I watched the swarm of moths and mosquitoes form like whirls of white wind around the bulbs.

"Who has seen the wind?" I said out loud, remembering a poem from a book Beatrice used to read to me in her rocking chair when I was a child. And suddenly I didn't want the emporium to close. I wanted everything to be the same as it had always been.

"Yes, Benny," my mother was saying softly. Her hand was on his arm. "You are family."

And almost twenty-three years later I could no longer remember who else was in the back room with us that night, or the way they looked, or what they said. But as I sat on the roof beside my son, I still knew the smell of Mr. Levine's watermelon rag. I knew the heat of that August night in Atlanta. The dark beyond the screen. The pride I'd felt, and the sadness, when others echoed my father's words: "This is family."

Remember this night, I'd told myself. And I studied the table covered with newspapers and the sound of the watermelon popping open and the spread of the juice as it soaked into an article in the *Atlanta Constitution* about a young pianist named Van Cliburn who had just won a prize in Russia.

And I smelled the aromas not only of the watermelons, but also the sugar cane leaning against the door and the pumpkins that would ripen in the fall and the licorice sticks melting in the heat of the jars that Mr. Levine always kept on his front counter.

And after a while I watched my father nod at Mr. Levine. I watched him stretch his arms across the backs of my chair and Mother's chair as though he wanted to gather us and the whole fruit emporium into his embrace. And I waited for Daddy to say whatever needed saying to this man and to the other people in the back room with us that night who had become part of our family. I knew he would tell us some story from *How to Win Friends and Influence People*. Share a bit of Carnegie wisdom that would explain the *whys* and *if onlys*. That would assure us that no matter what might happen, everything would be all right in the end.

"Yeah?" Jimmy asked.

"Yes. But your granddaddy only said, 'Huh.' "

I listened to Jimmy's sigh, and I looked off into the distance, to the skyline of downtown Atlanta lit up like a million candles. I imagined myself returning to his father's office, doing it right this time. When Miss Grimsley came to take me away, I would stand up with my shoulders straight and reach across the desk to shake Peter's hand.

"Oh, Jimmy," I said. "I wish you could have been with us at Mr. Levine's that night. You would have been so proud of your grandfather. His voice absolutely *resounded* with grace and dignity. 'Well,' he added, 'I guess you have to do what you think you need to do, Benny. But we'll hate like hell to see you go . . .' "

———

For a while my son sat motionless, silent, deep in thought.

"So, you see, Jimmy?" I finally said, seizing the moment. "Happiness doesn't depend on who you are or what you have; it depends solely on—"

"Shhh," he whispered. "Do you feel something?"

No. I felt the wind blowing through my thin cotton blouse. I felt the weight of his boot against my ankle.

"Listen," he whispered. "Don't you feel her, too?"

I reached out and touched his hatchet earring. I ran my hand over the shaved side of his head. And I waited quietly beside him until he sighed again. Until he brushed an imaginary strand of hair from his forehead and asked, "So what do we do now, Mom?"

What I wanted to do was put my arms around him and hold on

for dear life. What I did instead was tell him to get off his fanny and help his poor mother up so she could go back to the chimney and make sure the blanket was still tucked around Harold.

———

"That was it?" Jimmy asked me this morning after we'd gotten down off the roof. His voice dripped with pity for a mother who has such a terrible time coming up with good endings. "That thing about the fruit place was the story you'd always meant to tell me?"

"Yes."

Harold chuckled. "Uh-huh," he said, continuing with the family history he'd been instructing my son on before being interrupted. "Your mama been this way since she was born. 'Likes to exaggerate her miseries,' is how Miz Matthews in there tells it. And that's the truth, sure enough. Lord Jesus! Trying to scare me into thinking she was going to jump. Why, your mama be the last person on earth to ever do a thing like that."

"Harold!" we heard Ida calling from the other room. "Have you gone and lost your mind?"

Harold grinned and finished putting Babs' *Book of Lists* toilet paper on the roller for me: "20 Achievers at an Advanced Age."

"Margaret!" Ida called. "Come in here, quick! You need to read this!"

Jimmy and I looked at each other and smiled.

We found Ida where we knew she'd be, standing by the window staring through the telescopic lens of Jimmy's camera.

"I can't believe it!" she cried, without taking her eyes away.

I shoved her aside so I could see for myself. The sky was still cloudy with the threat of rain. Sooner or later, Ida's roof would be washed clean. But as I read the message Harold and I had left behind for Katherine and Margaret and Minevah, for Leticia and Charlotte and Meg, it occurred to me that if I was lucky for a change there might be just enough red clay mixed in with the leaves and lichen, the pine needles and dogwood blossoms, to make it impossible to remove all the stains from Arnold's antique cedar shingles.

"I don't know what gets into you sometimes," Miss Tinkerbell said, sighing. "Is that what you really meant to write?"

In my mind's eye, I visualized her mouth gaping open in amazement. I heard the laughter rising in her throat.

M-A-R-G-A-R-E-T

W-A-S

H-E-R-E

"Yes."